THE WINDS OF WINTER

In the four years since she had left her husband David, Anne Metcalf had changed out of all recognition. So if she altered her appearance still more, and used an assumed name, was it possible that David would not recognise her? For she just *had* to go to his house to discover if what she suspected was true ...

THE WINDS OF WINTER

BY

SANDRA FIELD

MILLS & BOON LIMITED
15–16 BROOK'S MEWS
LONDON W1A 1DR

CHAPTER ONE

ANNE METCALFE left the hospital by the side door, buttoning up her coat as she went. The ice-cold wind nipped her fingers, and she fumbled for her gloves.

'Afternoon, Miss Metcalfe.'

She looked up and smiled at the commissionaire. 'Hi, Mr Soames. Brr, isn't it cold?'

'It is that. Winter's here to stay, I'm afraid. Too cold to be without a hat.'

She wrinkled her nose at him, amused by his avuncular attitude; he was a favourite of all the nurses. 'I was late for work this morning, so I forgot it.'

'Tch, tch ... Well, have a nice lunch, miss.' He raised his gloved hand in salute, his faded blue eyes lingering appreciatively on the rich brown hair that tumbled over her collar, and on the delicate beauty of her features. Lovely girl, Miss Metcalfe, but sad-looking somehow. He'd often wondered why, but there was something about her that made it impossible to ask.

Anne walked quickly down the driveway to the main road, pulling her collar up around her ears. Mr Soames was right, it was too cold to be without a hat. He was a dear—and she had noticed how he, like nearly all of her colleagues at the hospital, called her Miss Metcalfe, rather than Mrs Metcalfe. Other than the nursing superintendent, very few knew of her brief, disastrous marriage. She shivered from more than the cold, and deliberately began thinking about her theatre date with Jonathan tonight; she would wear the long dark green skirt and the new blouse she had bought last week.

Within a few minutes she had walked across the park to join the lunch-hour crowds on the sidewalks of Spring Garden Road. Perhaps because it was a cold day, or per-

haps because she had woken up with what she called the
January blues, she suddenly decided to treat herself today
—rather than her usual rushed sandwich and coffee at a
lunch counter, she would go to Pierre's and have something
a little special. She pushed open the door of the restaurant
and went into the foyer. A cheerful log fire burned in the
fireplace and there was a twinkle of candles on the red-
checked tablecloths. There was also a line-up of people
waiting to be seated. Well, she had an hour ... as she
waited, she amused herself by studying the occupants of
the nearest tables, until she came to a small corner table by
the fire. There was a girl seated there alone, reading a
magazine with an intense concentration that immediately
struck a chord in Anne's memory. Of course—it was
Marianne, Marianne Winters, her old friend of nursing
school days. Impetuously she left the queue and threaded
her way among the tables.

'Hi, Marianne! Remember me?'

The girl looked up and Anne smiled to herself: the
same curly brown hair and madcap green eyes, the same
dimpled cheeks. She waited for the well-remembered
sparkle of Marianne's smile, a smile that had led more than
one serious-minded intern into trouble.

But Marianne, far from smiling, was looking distinctly
puzzled 'I—I'm sorry. Should I remember you?'

Anne's jaw dropped. 'It's Anne—well, I'm Anne Metcalfe now, but I was Anne Brown when I first knew you.
We were students together in Montreal.'

'Anne?' Marianne gazed at the other girl with something
approaching consternation. 'Why, so it is! Goodness, I
didn't recognise you at all.' Belatedly recalling her manners,
she added, 'Please sit down and join me.'

As Anne slipped out of her coat and deposited her handbag on the floor, she could still sense the bewilderment in
her friend's face. 'Have I changed that much?' she asked,
half jokingly.

'Yes, you have. I could have passed you in the street and
not known you.'

'Well, it's been what—four or five years since we've seen each other?'

'I left Montreal right after you left nursing school to get married—so it's five years. It seems a long time ago, doesn't it?'

'Yes,' Anne said shortly, tracing a pattern on the table-cloth with her fingernail and beginning to wonder if it had been a good idea to make herself known to her old friend again. She was glad of the diversion when the waitress arrived to take their orders.

But Marianne had not been deflected. 'What on earth are you doing down here—and how's David?'

There was a little silence.

'Something's wrong, isn't it?' Marianne asked gently. For all her impetuous ways, she had always been sensitive to the troubles of others: it was one of her most endearing traits.

'Yes.' Anne looked up, meeting the other girl's gaze with bleak grey eyes. 'I'm working at the general hospital—men's surgical ward—I took my final year of training here in Halifax, and then went to work right afterwards. That's three years ago now.'

'And David?'

'David and I . . . don't live together any more.'

'Oh dear, I *am* sorry!' Marianne patted the other girl's hand. 'But didn't I hear that you were pregnant?'

'Yes,' Anne replied in a low voice. 'The baby died.'

There was genuine distress in Marianne's green eyes. 'There's nothing much I can say, is there? Except how dreadfully sorry I am. Was it—very bad?'

'Yes, it was very bad.' Bravely Anne raised her head. 'But it's over now, and I try not to think about it too much. What's the use, after all?'

'Are you divorced?'

'No.'

'Do you see David at all?'

'I haven't laid eyes on him since the baby was born. And I don't want to!'

'But Anne, surely one day you'll want to remarry? You're far too gorgeous to stay in limbo for ever! If you and David are really finished, isn't the sensible thing to get a divorce? And then get on with a new life?'

It all sounded too reminiscent of what Jonathan had suggested on more than one occasion. 'I suppose I should. But I don't think I could bear to see David again, or to get in touch with him——'

'You're still in love with him?'

Anne blinked in surprise. 'No! Of course not. The exact opposite, in fact—I hate him! And I hate what he did to me—that's why I never want to see him again.'

'Oh.' Marianne digested this for a minute. 'Obviously he's not interested in remarrying, or he'd have been in touch with you.'

This aspect had never really occurred to Anne before. 'I suppose you're right. Mind you, he has no idea where I am ...'

The waitress put two steaming tureens of French onion soup in front of them, and a basket of hot rolls on the table. Absently buttering her bread, Anne gave a bitter little laugh. 'Why should he remarry anyway? He always got what he wanted from women without resorting to marriage.'

'Was that the problem—other women, I mean?'

'Oh, one of them.' Anne smiled wryly, although the smile did not reach her eyes. 'I'm sure you don't want to hear the whole sad story behind my marriage break-up. It's over now, and in the past ... And I'm starting to enjoy life in Halifax. I like my job, and I'm making new friends. So let's talk about you for a change—what have you been up to since I saw you last?'

Although it was fairly obvious that Marianne's curiosity was not satisfied, it was equally obvious that Anne had changed the subject. 'Well, after listening to you, I hardly like to say this, but——' a tender little smile played about Marianne's lips, 'I'm getting married next week and we're emigrating to Australia.'

'Marianne, how lovely! Tell me all about him.'

'He's a doctor—I always did have a weakness for the medical profession, didn't I? His name's Jim Blanchard, he's twenty-nine, tall, dark and handsome, and loves me to distraction.'

Marianne looked so pleased with herself that Anne couldn't help laughing. 'I think that's marvellous—congratulations! But I'm sorry you're leaving just when we've met again.'

'So am I. It's pure chance we ran into each other. I had no idea you were here. I worked in Fredericton for the past two years as the children's nurse at a day care centre—I'm only in Halifax for this last week. Jim's parents live here, and I'm staying with them. When Jim got the offer of this terrific job with the flying doctor service—his uncle is one of the directors—he felt he couldn't turn it down. It's only for a two-year term, and then I expect we'll come home again. Canada—especially the Maritimes—is really home for both of us.' Marianne glanced at her watch. 'Heavens! Is that the time? I've got to run. I'm meeting Jim's mother at Scotia Square for a last-minute shopping spree. Anne, I'd really like to see you again before I leave.' She paused and thought for a moment. 'Let's have dinner together one evening. How about Wednesday?'

'I'd like to do that.'

'Okay. We can meet at the new Greek restaurant a couple of blocks from here. Around seven?'

'I'll be there. See you then.'

' 'Bye!'

Quickly Anne finished her own meal, and hurried back to the hospital. She hung up her coat and went to the washroom to comb her hair; she wore it pinned under her cap while she was on duty. She was alone in the room and as she rinsed her hands she found herself staring in the mirror at her reflection. How greatly she must have changed for Marianne not to recognise her!

She cast her mind back and remembered the Anne of five years ago. Her hair had been short then, and for a while she had affected a frizzy Afro hairdo. She had even dyed it blonde at one stage. Her fingernails had been long, painted scarlet, her make-up had veered on the heavy side: lots of mascara and eyeshadow had been the younger Anne's idea of sophistication. How young she had been, that girl! And how foolish—in love with her husband, but dazzled by his money, his social position, and by the prestige of being the wife of David Metcalfe, the brilliant young defence lawyer. It had all gone to her head, and like a vividly coloured butterfly she had fluttered and danced her way through the days, filling them with pleasure and fun.

The other Anne grimaced at herself in the mirror. It had taken a long time for her hair to grow into its present silken smoothness, a warm brown with auburn highlights, after the way she had tortured and frizzed it; her nails, tipping the same slender fingers, were neatly trimmed and polished a pale pink now. Obvious changes, these. The ones Anne did not fully recognise were more subtle. Her figure was fuller, and she moved with a grace she had lacked in those days. Her face, fined down by the suffering she had undergone, had a mature beauty in its curve of cheek and sweep of dark eyebrow. But it was her eyes that held one's attention. They were chameleon eyes, a smoky grey in some lights, a forest green in others; always in their depths lurked a incalculable sadness that time had not erased.

The locker room door swung open. 'Hi, Anne! Can you change Mr Woodside's dressing for me? He particularly asked for you. And he gets so grumpy if I try to do it.'

Pinning her cap into place, Anne smiled at the other nurse. 'Sure, no problem. Although I don't know what's so special about me.' The ward, with its myriad duties, soon swallowed her up, giving her no time to brood over the past and all its bitter memories.

Jonathan called for her a little before eight. As the bell rang, she was just fastening her earring, a tiny gold loop set with a jade droplet. Jonathan had bought them for her in Toronto. He travelled a lot, because he owned and operated an art gallery in downtown Halifax, dealing only with Canadian artists; she knew he was becoming well known for his flair in discovering new talent and for his innate good taste.

He bent and kissed her. 'You're looking very lovely.'

'Thank you.' She had taken trouble with her appearance, perhaps in an obscure desire to banish the memories the day had aroused. She was wearing a full-length skirt of dark green wool, of a simple design yet a fluidity of line that was very becoming; she had teamed it with a tailored shirt of figured Thai silk and a gold necklace; her eyes gleamed green under her smoothly upswept hairdo.

As she put on her second earring, she surveyed Jonathan affectionately. He had been a good friend for well over a year now. He was not much taller than she, stocky in build rather than lean; he was by no means handsome, but his undistinguished features were lit by a kindness and inner integrity that had attracted Anne from the first time she met him. His hair was blond, with a tendency to stand on end. His eyes were his best feature—they were a warm dark brown and saw rather more than most people gave him credit for.

He took her black evening cloak from the hanger and put it over her shoulders. 'Ready?'

'Mmm——' She peered in her bag. 'Have I got my key? Oh, there it is.'

The play was a delightful Noël Coward comedy; afterwards they had a cocktail and a light meal in one of the restaurants that overlooked the harbour, where the moon shone slickly on the black water. By the time Jonathan drove her home it was nearly midnight. 'Will you come in for a coffee?' she asked, rather hoping he would say no. It had been a long day and she was tired.

'Okay—thanks.'

As she unlocked the door, she suggested, 'Why don't you light the fire in the living-room and put on some music, while I fix the coffee?'

When she entered the living-room a few minutes later,

he was relaxing in the armchair by the fire, looking very much at home. Anne was proud of her apartment, and considered herself lucky to be able to afford it; it was one of two flats on the ground floor of an older home near the hospital and its windows overlooked hedges and a large garden, that in summer was shaded by tall elms. Because the rooms were oddly shaped they possessed a certain charm lacking in more modern apartment buildings. The atmosphere was comfortable and cosy. But as she added cream and sugar to Jonathan's coffee, she found herself wishing he did not look quite so much at home. For the past few weeks she had had the uneasy feeling that he wanted their easygoing relationship to change in some way ... on purpose she now tried to keep the conversation on trivial subjects and was chattering away about her new cross-country skis when she happened to look up and find his eyes on her, a quizzical look in their depths: he knew exactly what she was up to. She blushed and fell silent, burying her face in her coffee mug.

'Anne,' he said quietly, 'I want to talk to you.'

She nodded, unable to think of anything to say. He patted the arm of his chair. 'Come over here—you're too far away.'

Uncertainly she perched on the edge of the chair, her hands tightly clasped. In an absent-minded way Jonathan began to fondle them, his dark eyes trained on her face, where the firelight flickered over her creamy skin. 'I want to tell you—I—oh, hell, I rehearsed all kinds of fancy speeches, Anne, but all I want to say is that I'm in love with you.'

'Oh, Jonathan——'

'I've been sure of my feelings for some time now. You're a beautiful woman, my dear. Beautiful to look at'—he stroked a stray wisp of hair that curled against her neck, his hand unsteady—'and just as beautiful inside.'

He paused expectantly and she murmured, staring down at their interlocked hands, 'That's sweet of you, Jonathan. But——'

'Anne, will you marry me?' he blurted.

Distressed, she said, 'Jonathan, you know I can't. I'm already married, you've known that since we met.'

'You're not married in any sense but the legal one and you know it! You haven't even seen the man for four years—and you call that marriage?'

She tried to lighten the atmosphere. 'Just the same, the courts call it marriage and I don't think I'm cut out to be a bigamist!'

'The courts also have something they call divorce. And after four years it's very easy to obtain.'

'No!' The exclamation was torn from her.

'Why not? Don't tell me you're still in love with your husband?'

This was the second time today someone had accused her of that. Every fibre of her being rose up to repudiate it. 'I am not in love with my husband,' she said, spacing each word with clarity, 'but I cannot bear the thought of getting in touch with him for a divorce, or even of ever seeing him again. I hate him—don't you understand? I hate him!'

Her fingers clenched in the soft fabric of her skirt and gently Jonathan loosened them. 'Okay,' he said mildly, 'I believe you. But you don't have to see him, Anne, or get in touch with him directly—it can all be done through lawyers.'

'He'd have to appear in court.'

'Well—I suppose so.'

'I just can't do it, Jonathan.' Her breath caught in her throat in a tiny sob. 'I don't expect you to understand—I'm not sure I understand myself. I only know that I never want to see him again.'

'No, I don't understand. You've never told me what happened between the two of you or why you split up.'

'I'm trying to forget it,' she said in a low voice.

'So what are you going to do?' he persisted, an unusual edge to his tone. 'Live alone for the rest of your life? Married but not married? You can't condemn yourself to that kind of an existence!'

'I've managed very well for the past four years,' she said with a kind of desperate pride.

'Sure you have—but that doesn't mean you can continue that way indefinitely. 'You're young and beautiful and intelligent—and you're capable of great depths of loving, I know that. You can't live like a nun, Anne. Apart from anything else, don't you ever want to have children?'

She flinched as though he had struck her, and a sheen of tears blurred her vision. She had had a child, and the child had died—and because of that her husband had totally rejected her. Suddenly, it was all too much. She slid to her knees beside Jonathan's chair and began to cry. Great rasping sobs tore at her throat, her shoulders shaking with the intensity of her grief. David . . . and the baby she had never seen . . . for a while she had had so much, and now she had nothing . . .

Jonathan held her quietly, his hands gentle on her shuddering form, until gradually her sobbing lessened. He pushed a handkerchief into her hand and said flatly, 'I'm going to pour you a drink—stay there.'

He came back in a few minutes with two brandy snifters, the liquid amber in the crystal goblets. 'Drink up,' he ordered.

Anne had blown her nose and wiped her face while he was gone, and now she took a gulp of the brandy, feeling its warmth creep down her throat. 'That's better,' she said shakily.

'Okay. And now you're going to tell me just what happened four years ago, Anne.'

This was a new Jonathan. He was not normally the dictatorial type. Besides, there was no fight left in her, and he did deserve to hear the truth.

'I have to start earlier than four years ago,' she said slowly, staring into the dancing flames. 'It all started long before that . . . I think I told you once before that my parents came to Canada from England when I was very young. They both died in a 'flu epidemic when I was three. There were no other relatives, so I was put in an orphanage and from there in a series of foster-homes. I never felt loved—nobody really cared what happened to me—and I never had any money of my own. You have no idea how good it feels now just to have a job of my own and pay my own way——'

Jonathan got up to put another log in the fire, and idly she watched the sparks shoot up the chimney, their brief, bright light soon extinguished in the blackness. Her happiness with David had been that brief . . .

'So how did you get in training for nursing?'

'That was a stroke of pure luck. My last foster-home was by far the best. I went there when I was sixteen. Mrs Knowles—I called her Madge—was the head nurse in the children's ward in a hospital in Montreal. At first she got me on their volunteer staff; they had teenagers in to read to the children and play games with them. I loved it so much that she helped me to enrol as a student nurse, and saw to it that I had enough money while I studied. I owe her such a lot. We still write regularly.'

'But you didn't finish your training there, did you?'

'No—Madge was furious.' The girl's face softened, lit by an inner light that made Jonathan obscurely jealous. 'I met David at the annual Christmas dance—he was on the Board of Directors of the hospital. And that was that. Two months later we were married.'

'How old were you?'

'Not quite nineteen.' She took a sip of brandy, and sighed. 'Hindsight—it's so easy to look back and see where things went wrong. I loved David—loved him passionately, and we had some wonderful times together. But I was young and flighty and it all went to my head—his huge house, the servants, the three cars, the never-ending social whirl. I loved it all—and somewhere in the excitement Anne and David got lost. He started going to parties without me and I started doing the same. Then I heard his name coupled with someone else's and we had a terrible quarrel. Purely to spite him, I went skiing with his best friend—oh, Jonathan, it all sounds so silly and tawdry now . . .'

'But at the time you were badly hurt.'

'Yes—and frightened too. I think after all the upsets of my childhood I saw David as security. He was mine. I needed that feeling of security so badly and suddenly even that was being snatched away. With him gone, I knew I'd have nothing.'

'That's understandable.'

'Oh, it is now. But at the time I don't think I understood what was going on. I just knew I was miserable, and the more miserable I felt, the more I flailed out at him, and the more I filled my life with parties and people and a frantic search for fun. I'd never want to go through that again.' She shivered. 'I was horribly jealous too—I couldn't stand to see him with another woman.'

She shifted her position, her burnished head on Jonathan's knee. 'Matters weren't helped by his mother, either— she resented me from the start. She had wanted David to make an advantageous marriage, choosing someone from his own social class, someone with family and money and the right background. Instead of which he married a penniless student nurse without a relative in the world, a little nobody from nowhere—and that's a direct quote. Claire frightened me. I used to think she'd stop at nothing to get rid of me.'

'What did happen in the end?'

'I discovered I was pregnant. I kept it a secret for as long as I could, because we hadn't planned to have children. But his mother found out and told David. I guess she thought it would drive us apart. She was wrong, though—for a while everything was all right again. He was pleased about the baby and we were closer together than we'd been for months. But then things began to go wrong again—David withdrew from me, and started doing a lot of travelling and when he was home he made sure there were always lots of people around. I didn't know what was the matter ... finally about two weeks before the baby was due, he announced he had a business trip to the States that he couldn't put off ...'

Her voice trailed away. As though it was yesterday she

was back in the drawing-room at David's country house on the shores of the St Lawrence. She could see the heavy gold curtains, the cream-coloured rug, the exquisitely crafted furniture ... and she could hear his voice echoing in her ears ...

'I'm leaving on the early morning flight from Ottawa.'

'Oh, David, do you have to go now?'

'Yes, it's unavoidable.'

'But the baby's nearly due.'

He bent his tawny head to light a cigarette, his voice indifferent to the point of insolence. 'That's hardly my problem.'

Anne had never learned to control her temper. 'I would have said it was very much your problem.'

'Do explain why,' he said with silky arrogance, his blue eyes like chips of ice, the sensual line of his mouth tight-held.

Taken aback, she sputtered, 'Well, it's your child, too.'

'Is it, my dear?'

The colour drained from her face, and unconsciously she gripped the edge of the piano for support. 'Of course it is! Whatever do you mean?'

'You spent a weekend skiing in the Laurentians with Ralph—or have you conveniently forgotten that? It's almost exactly nine months ago, isn't it?'

Appalled, she protested, 'David, there was a whole group of us there. You can't be insinuating——'

'Insinuating, hell!' In two swift strides he reached her, gripping her by the arms with cruel fingers. 'I'm not insinuating anything—I'm stating it as a fact. The child could be mine; it could equally well be Ralph's. For all I know there might be other possibilities. You weren't around home much then, were you?'

'Your mother's been talking to you,' she accused, sensing a woman's tortuous hand in this nightmare.

'Certainly it was my mother who pointed out the coincidence of the dates—but it was I who came to the regrettable conclusion that the child you're carrying might not be mine.'

'That's a filthy thing to say!'

'It was a filthy thing to do.'

She made one last effort, striving to keep the anger out of her voice. 'David, I swear to you that nothing ever happened between Ralph and me. I'm sorry I went away with him like that, it was a silly thing to do. But I was angry with you and I didn't stop to think.'

'That's the truest word you've said yet. You never do stop to think.' His blue eyes, rinsed clear of any emotion except contempt, raked her swollen figure. 'Well, you'll have two weeks to think about it now. Because I guess we'll just have to wait and see, won't we, dear wife? Whether your child has black hair, like Ralph, or fair hair, like your husband's. But don't expect me to sit around holding your hand while we do wait.'

'You're despicable!' she shrilled. 'I hate you—do you hear me? I hate you!'

He shook her, his eyes ablaze with such a primitive surge of fury that she shrank away from him, terrified by the unmasked violence in his face.

'I'm beginning to feel that it's entirely mutual,' he grated. 'How can I feel anything but hatred for a little tramp like you?' For a moment his eyes were anguished. 'How could you do it, Anne, how could you?'

'I didn't,' she said stonily.

He released her, running his fingers through his thick blond hair in a gesture of utter frustration. 'I'll be back in ten or twelve days. My mother will be staying here until I get back, so you won't be on your own.' He turned on his heel and strode out of the room, shutting the door behind him with an air of absolute finality. She had not seen him again.

The child was born four days later. Because she had been too listless and unhappy to take proper care of herself, Anne developed a severe cold which had turned into a mild form of pneumonia. She had had a long and difficult labour and, weakened by her illness, had been anaesthetised for the actual birth. Afterwards, fever and delirium had claimed her, and it was over a week before she fully regained consciousness. When she opened her eyes, the first person she saw was Claire Metcalfe, her mother-in-law. The older woman was sitting ramrod-straight by the edge of the bed, her immaculately groomed figure bathed in the late afternoon sunlight, her lips a thin, straight line as she gazed out of the window.

Anne let her eyes wander around the room—a neat hospital room, with a bowl of daffodils on the dresser. She felt a strange floating sensation and she had lost all sense of time. It seemed aeons ago that Claire had brought her to the hospital. She flexed her legs, sensing how weak she was. 'Claire?' she murmured.

The other woman swivelled in the chair. 'Ah, you're awake.'

'What day is it?'

'Thursday.'

'Thursday? But I came here on a Friday. It can't be Thursday!'

'You've been ill.'

Claire's manner was so hostile that Anne was repelled. Weakly she asked, 'David—has he been in to see me?'

'No.'

The monosyllable hung in the air. Suddenly fear struck the girl, fear such as she had never known before. 'Is he all right? Nothing's happened to him, has it?'

'He's perfectly all right.'

'Oh. . . .' Anne expelled her breath in a long sigh of relief. Her hands were resting on her flat stomach, and in quick delight she asked, 'Has he seen the baby? I don't even know what I had—is it a boy or a girl?'

There was a long silence. Claire looked down at her diamond-encrusted fingers, loosely clasped in her lap.

'Claire? Please——' Panic tightened Anne's voice. 'Something's wrong, isn't it? Tell me—please tell me!'

With a complete lack of emotion her mother-in-law said,

'The child was stillborn. I told you that you weren't taking proper care of yourself.'

Only later did Anne recognise the calculated cruelty behind Claire's manner. Now all she could do was gasp, 'Dead? You mean the baby's dead?'

'Yes.'

The room began to swirl around her. Fiercely she fought back the wave of dizziness. 'Was it a boy or a girl?'

'Does it matter?'

'It matters to me.'

'If you must know, it was a girl.'

Anne thrust her fist into her mouth to prevent herself from crying out loud. 'David—I need to see David,' she begged.

Calmly Claire got up from the chair and walked over to the window, her slim figure silhouetted against the evening sky. 'David will not be coming to see you,' she said precisely.

The girl closed her eyes, fighting for breath. 'Why not?'

'He asked me to give you a message. He's through with you—finished. He does not wish to see you again. He'll arrange a monthly income for you which will support you in far better style than I feel you deserve. However, that's his business. The gist of his message is that he doesn't want you back—ever again.'

In a furious burst of defiance Anne said, 'The child was his!'

'I'm really not interested in the paternity of your child. My job was to deliver a message, and I've done so.'

'Didn't he have the courage to deliver it himself?' Anne said bitterly.

'I can only assume he preferred not to see you again.'

Anne swallowed her pride in one last frantic effort. 'Claire, I beg of you, tell David I need to see him. I love him and I'm sure he still loves me. Somehow we should be able to save our marriage.'

'Very well, I shall tell him. But if I were you, I wouldn't set my hopes too high.' Calmly Claire put on her fur coat, and adjusted her hat in the mirror, as though she had just completed a normal social call. As she pulled on her suede gloves she added, 'I don't suppose I shall see you again. David's lawyer will come to the hospital in the next couple of days to make all the necessary arrangements.' She turned to face the girl, unable to prevent the glow of triumph in her cold blue eyes. 'Goodbye, Anne.'

CHAPTER TWO

A LOG crashed in the fireplace, sending a shower of sparks into the air. With a jerk Anne came back to the present. Confused, she brushed her hand over her eyes.

'You were a long way away.'

'Oh, Jonathan, I'm sorry!'

'Want to tell me about it?'

He deserved at least an abbreviated version of these dreadful days. 'David didn't think the child was his,' she said bluntly. 'He went away and I had to go to the hospital while he was gone.' Her voice quivered. 'The baby was born dead.'

Jonathan put an arm around her shoulders. 'My dear, I'm so sorry. Couldn't even that shared tragedy bring you together again?'

She gave a bitter little laugh. 'Far from it—David sent his mother to the hospital with the message that he didn't want to see me again. He was going to have a lawyer visit me to make financial arrangements. But I left before that could happen.'

'You mean you just walked out?'

'Yes. I saved my strength for a couple of days. Then I got dressed, waited until the duty nurses were having their coffee break, and walked out of the hospital. I caught a taxi to the airport, got a cash advance at the bank on my credit card, and went to the Air Canada desk. The first flight out with an empty seat was going to Halifax—so I bought a ticket under an assumed name and came here. As you know, I finished my nurse's training here and got a job. I've never heard from David since I left, nor do I want to.'

'It's an incredible story—it sounds to me as though you did the right thing to get out of that marriage.'

'I didn't know what else to do. And I was far too proud to take his money.'

'But, honey, that whole story only confirms my point of view. Sooner or later you'll have to get a divorce.'

'Oh, rationally, I know you're right,' she said with something like despair in her voice. 'But don't you see, Jonathan? I just can't bear the thought of getting in touch with him again. When I was ill in hospital I needed him so badly, and I begged him to come. But he didn't. When I needed him the most, he rejected me. I'll never forgive him for that.'

'Then all the more reason to cut the last tie that binds you together.'

Anne took a sip of brandy, feeling a great weariness overcome her. Jonathan was right. Of course he was right. But how could she do as he said? When she had first come to Halifax it had taken her months to get over the double agony of the failure of her marriage and the death of her child. But somehow she had managed. She had survived. Now Jonathan was asking her to reopen the wound, and she could not bear it. . . .

Jonathan carefully removed the goblet from her hands, placing it on the hearth. Chafing her cold fingers between his warm ones, he said gently, 'You look tired, honey.'

'Yes, I am. I didn't tell you this before, but I met an old friend at lunch time whom I hadn't seen since I was married—so you're the second person to bring back the past today.'

'And it's upset you.'

'Yes, it has.'

'I'll leave so you can go to bed. Before I go, will you promise me something?'

She nodded wordlessly.

'Think over everything I've said. I'm sure you'll come to realise that the only sensible thing is to get a divorce—and I'll help you in any way I can, and make it as easy as possible for you.' He raised her fingers to his lips. 'I love you, Anne, and I want to marry you. Remember that, too.'

Tears flooded her eyes again and she blinked them back. 'You're so kind, Jonathan, and you've been so good to me. I'm sorry I'm being difficult.'

'I'm sure we'll work it out.' He got up from the chair, pulling her to her feet. His arms encircled her waist and his lips found hers in a kiss of tender restraint that comforted her without arousing her in any way. 'I'll let myself out. Have a good sleep, dear, and I'll give you a call in a day or two.'

The surgical ward was exceptionally crowded the next few days, although Anne did not complain about this. It helped to keep her mind occupied and it tired her physically. Even so, the evenings seemed unbearably long and she was not sleeping well. Between them, Marianne and Jonathan had called up the ghosts of the past, ghosts which now haunted her day and night, refusing to be exorcised. She found herself recalling every detail of David's face: the lean line of his cheek, his deepset, brilliant blue eyes, his chiselled lips. For the first time in months she remembered their passionate hunger for each other, which lovemaking would only temporarily appease. She remembered the hard length of his muscled thighs, the breadth of his shoulders ... the sureness of his hands on her flesh, the fire his lips could ignite in her body. Even in the worst of their quarrels, she would melt at his touch. . . .

Inevitably this led her to thoughts of Jonathan—kind, dependable Jonathan, whose kisses had never excited her in the least, and whose embrace offered security rather than passion. How could she marry him, knowing what was lacking?

Yet for all their tempestuous lovemaking, she and David had been unable to live together. Time and again they had wounded each other, until his final, bitter rejection had ended the travesty of their marriage. So perhaps she would be happier married to Jonathan; perhaps passion was no basis for a marriage. Maybe Jonathan's undemanding companionship would offer a firmer foundation. . . .

Although her thoughts chased each other round and

round in her head as the days went by, she came no nearer
to any kind of a decision. On the weekend she and Jonathan
went for a drive in the country; he was leaving for Vancouver on the Sunday evening. Seeing the strain in her face,
he wisely and to her great relief, kept the conversation on
neutral grounds.

Back to work on Monday. And then it was Tuesday, a
day that was to change Anne's life for ever.

It began like any other. A brisk walk to work on snow-
caked pavement. The morning routine of bed-baths and
back-rubs and doctors' rounds. Lunch in the cafeteria.
Later in the afternoon she made a point to drop in and see
Mr Woodside, the crusty old gentleman who always re-
quested that Anne change his dressing. He was going home
today.

He thrust an envelope in her hands, saying gruffly, 'Buy
yourself something pretty.'

'That's sweet of you—but really, I can't take anything,
Mr Woodside.'

' 'Course you can. I won't tell that hatchet-faced head
nurse—what's her name? Miss Hallen?'

Inwardly Anne chuckled at this cavalier description of
her boss, even as she sensed that his feelings would be hurt
if she didn't accept his gift. 'Thank you,' she said awkwardly. 'It's very kind of you.'

'Nonsense! Wish I could do more for you than that. Got
a young man?'

She gasped, amused by his effrontery. 'Yes—no—I don't
know.'

'Well, don't marry him if you're not sure,' he pro-
nounced, staring at her from under bushy white eyebrows.
'Take that pile of magazines while you're here, why don't
you? I'd rather you got them than Miss Hatchet or whatever her name is.'

Unable to argue, Anne picked up the magazines. Impulsively she dropped a kiss on his withered cheek. 'Thank
you for that advice,' she said. 'I think perhaps you're
right.'

'Of course I am. You'll know when Mr Right comes

along. Now, off with you, girl. Got to get smartened up
before my wife comes for me. Swept me off my feet forty
years ago, she did, and I've never regretted it. Make sure
the same happens to you.'

Smothering an almost hysterical desire to giggle, Anne
left the room. She tucked the envelope in her handbag and
shoved the magazines into her locker—she'd glance through
them tonight. Cantankerous old man! But oddly she felt he
was right. She couldn't marry Jonathan. The truth was, it
was David who had swept her off her feet so many years
ago—and what would Mr Woodside say about that?

It was nearly nine o'clock that evening before she
settled into the armchair by the fire, a mug of cocoa beside
her and the armload of magazines in her lap. She had
bought groceries after work, vacuumed the apartment, and
then had had a shower, changing into a long red velvet
housecoat. Now she felt strangely at peace with herself, all
the problems of the past few days in abeyance.

She shuffled through the magazines until she came to this
month's issue of one which dealt exclusively with the
Atlantic provinces; it was a glossy and attractive periodical,
its articles and coloured photographs artistically arranged
to best effect. One entire section was devoted to Prince
Edward Island, the fertile, crescent-shaped island that lay
in the Northumberland Strait off New Brunswick. Anne
had often wanted to go there; she must make a point of doing so this summer, she decided. Contentedly she began to
read, slowly flipping the pages.

His name leaped out at her from the black and white
print. 'Mr David Metcalfe, Stornaway, Prince Edward
Island.' For a moment she was literally paralysed, every
nerve ending frozen with shock.

Then her heart began to pound in her breast. Her hands
were shaking so badly that the magazine slipped from her
grasp and fell to the floor. Frantically she picked it up,
almost tearing the pages in her haste to find his name again.
There—Mr David Metcalfe. . . .

It was an advertisement, and she had to read it at least

three times before its implications began to penetrate her whirling brain. 'Companion required for young child. Hours irregular, applicant must be over 21 years of age, with some professional training beyond the high school level. Second language preferable although not essential. Room and board supplied, salary negotiable depending on qualifications. References required.'

In the lower right-hand corner of the advertisement was the name of David Metcalfe and the Prince Edward Island address. The opposite corner read: 'Apply in writing or by telephone to Mrs Henriette Gould, Suite 510, Morton Building, Halifax, Nova Scotia.' A local telephone number followed.

Stunned, her first reaction was that it couldn't be David —not her David. Metcalfe, while not a common name, was not so uncommon that there could not be two David Metcalfes. And David, when she had left, was living either in his Montreal apartment or at Tall Trees, his country estate a few miles outside the city. He had never, as far as she knew, owned or expressed any desire to own property on the Island.

Furthermore, since he had not remarried, it was impossible that he should be looking for a housekeeper for a young child in his care. It couldn't be David; it couldn't be.

But what if it was? There was no real reason for him to remain in the Montreal area; his work was such that he could live wherever he chose. Had he adopted a child? Or had he become involved with a woman who already had a young child?

Knife-sharp, jealousy ripped through her and she was horrified to find her fingers shaking again. After his desertion of her and the long months of separation, how could it possibly matter to her what he did? She was free of him. . . .

Her earlier mood of contentment was shattered. Restless and confused, she paced up and down the living-room like a caged animal. It was humiliating to find that the mere mention of a man's name could so disturb her. All the defences she had so carefully built up over the past four years had tumbled to the ground, totally ineffective against this unexpected onslaught. Her body ached with a need she dared not define; her eyes burned in her head.

Although she eventually went to bed, she slept hardly at all. In vivid and painful detail the events of her marriage paraded themselves through her tired brain. David's whirlwind courtship that had changed her mundane life to one of incredible and rapturous happiness ... the delicious fulfilment she had found in his arms ... the mad kaleidoscope of parties, glittering evenings at the symphony, trips to Toronto and New York. New clothes, fast cars. A neverending cycle of fun and frenetic excitement. Flirtations and quarrels ... reconciliations in the darkness of their bedroom, inevitably followed by more quarrels. All leading up to that final bitter repudiation that had changed her love to a hatred just as deep and passionate.

When she dressed for work the next morning, she tried to hide the ravages of the night with make-up, applying rouge to her wan cheeks, and hoping that eyeshadow and mascara would draw attention away from the dark circles under her eyes. Oh Lord, and today was the day she was dining with Marianne Winters—she'd never be able to deceive Marianne's all-too-sharp eyes. The last thing she did as she left the apartment was to tear the advertisement out of the magazine and thrust it into her handbag, although why she did this, she did not stop to think.

At ten-thirty she had her regular morning coffee break. Without conscious thought she found herself in the private telephone booth at the end of the corridor, holding the scrap of paper in her hand, staring at the telephone number given there. She had to know—she simply had to know.

Without any idea of what she was going to say, she slipped a dime into the slot and waited for the dial tone. Clumsily she dialled the seven numbers. Her mouth dry, she heard the telephone begin to ring.

'Houston and Tompkins, Barristers. Good morning.' A crisp female voice.

'Oh—er—good morning. Is a Mrs Henriette Gould there, please?'

'Yes, one moment, please, and I'll put you through.'

There was a series of clicks. 'Henriette Gould speaking.'

Her mind a blank, Anne fumbled for words. 'I—I saw your advertisement in the *Atlantic Herald*. I wondered if you'd mind telling me a little more about the job. I'm not sure whether I want to apply or not.'

'Certainly. Who is this speaking, please?'

Impossible to give her own name. She said the first words that came into her head. 'Marianne Winters.'

'As the advertisement states, Miss Winters, the position is one of companion rather than housekeeper; no housework is involved. It's a live-in position. Stornaway is a small village on the north shore of Prince Edward Island, and Mr Metcalfe's home is a very substantial one—I'm sure you'd be most comfortable.'

'I see,' Anne said slowly, wondering how she could get to the crux of the matter.

'May I ask what your qualifications are?'

'I'm a registered nurse and I speak French fluently'— this thanks to her years in Montreal.

'That sounds most suitable.'

Not caring how odd her question might sound, Anne asked, 'Mr Metcalfe, is he from Prince Edward Island?'

'No, he moved there very recently from Montreal.'

She swallowed. 'And the child—is it a boy or a girl?'

'A little girl. Her name is Jessica, and she's four years old.'

The world stopped. Anne blurted, 'Is it—his child?'

Mrs Gould's well-bred tones sounded faintly surprised. 'Well, of course. It's his daughter.'

Feeling as though a giant hand was mercilessly squeezing her heart, Anne strove for control. Somehow she had to end this nightmare conversation. From a long way away she heard her voice say, 'Thank you for talking to me, Mrs Gould. Perhaps I could think about it for a day or two, and get in touch with you then.'

'By all means, Miss Winters. We can always arrange an interview at a time that would be convenient for you.'

'Thank you. Goodbye.'

'Goodbye, Miss Winters.'

Weakly Anne leaned against the wall of the phone booth, breathing as hard as if she had just finished running a race. David—her husband—had a daughter. A four-year-old daughter whose name was Jessica Metcalfe. The words beat against her brain. Four years ago she, Anne, had given birth to a baby girl. David had been the father of that baby. So Jessica—Jessica must be hers. She had not died. A ripple of pure joy spread through her whole body. Her baby had not died ...

Someone tapped on the door of the booth. 'Are you okay, Anne?' It was one of the other nurses. 'If you're through, I'd like to make a call.'

'Oh, of course—sorry,' Anne stammered.

By an intense effort of concentration she somehow got through the rest of the morning, conscious always of that fugitive glow of happiness that with the slightest encouragement would burst into joyous flame. At lunch time, having absolutely no appetite for food, she pulled on her fur hat, buttoned up her heavy coat and started walking in the direction of Point Pleasant Park, at the tip of Halifax's peninsula. The stately pines welcomed her into their midst, casting their grey shadows on the snow. An Atlantic wind sharpened the air. She walked briskly along the winding trails between the trees, delighting in her new-found happiness. It was not until she arrived at the shoreline, where the grey seas sucked at the rocks, that she began belatedly to think.

Claire had told her that the baby was dead. So either Jessica was not her child, or Claire had lied. Why should she have lied? The answer was inescapable—because David had told her to. Oh God, Anne thought in anguish, how he must have hated me! How else could he have been so cruel? In one blow he had deprived her of husband and child. A sob tore at her throat and tears blurred her vision, so that leaden sky and grey sea merged into one.

With the swiftness of a blow, doubt struck her. David could not have been so brutal—not to his wife, whom once he had loved with all the intensity and passion of his nature. So perhaps, after all, it was not her child. Maybe after the tragic death of their baby, he had adopted a child ... After the joy she had experienced all morning, such a thought was intolerable.

She thrust her hands deep in her pockets. Head down against the wind, she began to walk back to work. She was reaching the limits of her endurance, and well she knew it. She was caught in a devastating dilemma—either David had deliberately lied to her or else the child was not hers. Both prospects seemed insupportable. By the time she reached the hospital her pain had coalesced into an unshakable conviction: somehow—and at the moment she had no idea how—she had to find out the truth. She would have no peace until she did.

It was not until she was seated across from Marianne in the restaurant that evening that the solution came to her, crystal clear in its simplicity. All she had to do was convince her friend. Her eyes a brilliant emerald green, she leaned forward. 'Marianne, I want you to do me a favour before you go. Rather an unusual favour.'

Her friend grinned goodnaturedly. 'Sure. What's up?'

Succinctly Anne explained about the advertisement and her subsequent conversation with Mrs Gould. 'There are only two choices,' she concluded. 'They lied about the baby—or Jessica isn't my child. Marianne, I have to know —you do see that, don't you?'

For once Marianne was speechless. She took a long sip of her wine. 'I can't believe it,' she said finally. 'Nobody could be that cruel.'

'If you follow that line of reasoning, it means Jessica is not my child.'

Marianne stared at her in consternation. 'Yes, that's right. You're absolutely right. You have to know, don't you? I can see that. How will you find out?'

'That's where the favour comes in. I want to apply for the job, Marianne. That way I can see Jessica—and I'm sure once I see her I'll know whether or not she's mine. But for obvious reasons I can't use my own name.' Anne crumbled her roll, her eyes on her friend. 'You're leaving for Australia in three days—will you let me use your name?' Marianne blinked, her mouth dropping open. Hurriedly Anne added, 'Before you answer, I guess I have a bit of a confession to make. When I was talking to Mrs Gould, she asked my name. Our dinner date was on my mind, so without thinking I used your name then. Truly it wasn't intentional—but now I have to admit it seems rather providential.'

'Anne, you're mad! You'll never get away with it!'

'Why not?' Eagerly she pressed her point. 'First of all, you and David have never met.'

'That's true enough.'

'And do you remember when we met the other day? You didn't recognise me, did you?'

'No—no, I didn't. But I'm not your husband.'

Anne grimaced, temporarily discouraged. 'Maybe I wouldn't have to see that much of him, he always used to travel a lot.'

'Anne, why is all this deceit necessary? Why can't you just go there and ring the doorbell and ask to see your child?'

'Because for one thing I don't know it is my child. And for another, I wouldn't give David the satisfaction of crawling back to him.'

'Oh dear, it is a muddle!'

'Yes,' Anne agreed quietly, her very quietness carrying conviction. 'I'll go mad if I don't find out the truth.'

'All right, I'll do it!' Mischief danced in Marianne's eyes as she raised her wine glass. 'To the new Marianne Winters!'

'Bless you!'

'You may not bless me before this is all over,' Marianne said wryly. 'But I guess as I'm in for a penny, I might as

well be in for a pound. You can have my driver's licence;
I won't be needing it where I'm going. And I have letters
of reference from my last two employers. You can have
them as well. On one condition—that you write to me and
let me know what happens. I'll be dying of curiosity.'

'Of course I will! And it's wonderful of you to do so
much.'

'I hope so,' Marianne said soberly. 'I just hope you won't
get hurt all over again, Anne. It's a very real possibility,
you know.'

Anne shrugged this aside. 'I can't help it. I won't rest
until I've found out the truth.' Eagerly she went on, 'Could
you tell me something about your last two jobs, in case I
get asked any awkward questions?'

So throughout the rest of the meal Marianne coached
her friend about her life in Fredericton. Finally she said,
'You've got it letter-perfect. So now what will you do—call
Mrs Gould tomorrow?'

'First thing, so that with luck I'll get an interview with
her right away. Just pray that no one else better qualified
than I is trying for the job.'

'I'm leaving on Saturday, so I'll give you the papers before then.' Marianne looked at her watch. 'I'm supposed to
meet Jim and his mother in a few minutes, we're going to
a gathering of a whole horde of aunts and uncles and
cousins. If I'd known he had so many relatives, I'd have
eloped!' Pulling on her gloves, she said seriously, 'Good
luck, Anne. I have a feeling you'll need it.'

'Thanks, Marianne. You've been a real friend.'

The interview went without a hitch, and three days later
Anne found out the job was hers. She and Mrs Gould
formalised the salary and travelling arrangements, and that
was that. Because there was a surplus of nurses, she was
only required to give a week's notice at the hospital; so in
just over a week she would be on her way to the Island ...
and to Jessica.

The ease of her transformation from Anne Metcalfe to

Marianne Winters had rather horrified her. She ought to be feeling qualms of conscience over the deception, she supposed, but because at some deep level she knew she was fighting for her very life, it was impossible to feel guilty. In fact, she was exultant at the way everything was falling into place. Mrs Gould had removed two major sources of worry: Claire Metcalfe, Anne's erstwhile mother-in-law, still resided in Montreal, life in Prince Edward Island apparently not being to her taste; and secondly, Anne's presence in Stornaway would be mainly required during David Metcalfe's frequent absences, and during these periods while he was away she would be, in effect, on duty twenty-four hours a day. : However, when he was home she would be free to go her own way. 'That's what the advertisement meant by "irregular hours",' Mrs Gould had said drily. 'You'd be surprised how many people were put off by that arrangement.' But to Anne, of course, it was a godsend— with a bit of luck, she might not have to meet David at all.

She spent her last week in Halifax shopping for sensible, dull-coloured tweed skirts and sweaters and equally sensible low-heeled shoes. She bought two pairs of glasses, one pair with tinted lenses; it was the only way she knew to disguise the tell-tale colour of her eyes. So preoccupied was she with all her preparations—for she also had to sublet her apartment—that one person's reaction to all this completely slipped her mind: Jonathan's. He had flown to Vancouver before she had even discovered the advertisement in the magazine; she had forgotten about his imminent return. When the doorbell rang one evening, two days before she was due to leave, she was in the living-room packing up her favourite ornaments and pictures to take with her. Boxes and tissue paper littered the floor. She looked down at herself ruefully. She was wearing her oldest jeans and a scoop-necked T-shirt and her hair was pulled back in a ponytail. Oh well . . .

She opened the door. 'Jonathan!' she exclaimed in consternation. 'Oh, heavens—come in.'

Immediately he saw the mess in the living-room. 'What's

up?' he said, amused. 'You look as though you're about to pull up stakes?'

She flushed scarlet, looking a picture of guilt. 'When did you get back?' she stammered.

'On the six-thirty flight.' He grinned at her boyishly. 'You should be flattered—I came straight here on the chance you'd be home. Well, aren't you even going to give me a kiss?'

Without doing as he asked, she said flatly, 'You'd better come in the living-room and sit down. I'll pour you a drink. I have a lot to tell you.'

The gravity of her tone forewarned him. 'What's up? Is something wrong?' His voice sharpened. 'Anne, aren't you going to marry me?'

For a moment she closed her eyes, wishing she were any-where but here. 'Things have changed, Jonathan.' She re-moved a pile of books from his favourite armchair and motioned for him to sit down. Forgetting all about her offer of a drink, she perched on the hassock, facing him. Unable to think of a way to break it to him gently, she plunged right into an explanation of the events of the past few days. 'So I'm leaving the day after tomorrow,' she concluded. 'According to Mrs Gould, David is tied up with a case in Toronto and won't be back for at least two weeks. By then I'll know whether Jessica's my daughter or not.'

Jonathan simply stared at her, an unaccustomedly bleak look in his brown eyes. 'Where's that drink?' he said heavily. 'I have a feeling I'm going to need it.'

Glad to escape, Anne went to the kitchen, reappearing with a Scotch and soda for him and a sherry for herself.

'I can't believe you're doing this,' he began without pre-amble. 'You've quit your job—and they're not so easy to come by nowadays. You've sublet this apartment. You're walking out on me. And all on the offchance that this child should turn out to be yours. It's crazy!'

'What do you mean—offchance?' she responded hotly. 'I'm almost sure she must be mine.'

'I'm glad you said "almost". I can think of any number

of other possibilities. And how are you going to know anyway? Are you expecting the child to rush up to you and call you "Mother"?'

Anne paled at the savagery in his tone. 'Of course not. I can't explain it to you, Jonathan, but if Jessica is my child, I'll know. I just will, that's all.'

'Feminine intuition, I suppose?'

'Jonathan, please!'

'Quite apart from any other considerations, what you're doing is illegal. Do you realise you're presenting yourself as someone else? The law takes a dim view of that kind of thing. It's just as well your friend Marianne has already gone to Australia—I'd like to give her a good shaking for encouraging you in this foolishness.'

'It's not foolishness! Jonathan, Jessica might be my daughter. Can't you understand what that means to me?'

He made a visible effort to get a grip on himself. 'Okay, I can see that. But in God's name, Anne, why all this rigmarole about applying for the job under a false name? If the child is yours, all you have to do is knock at the front door and ask your precious husband why the hell he deceived you four years ago. As a lawyer he should know that he can't get away with that kind of thing. It's that simple. Instead of which you've burned all your bridges and now you're off on a wild goose chase.'

Quite suddenly she recovered her sense of humour. 'And you're mixing your metaphors.'

He glared at her. Then reluctantly his face softened. 'Yeah, you're right. Damn it, Anne, I'm sorry. I really lost my cool, didn't I? My only excuse is that you took me by surprise.'

'It all happened so fast,' she said apologetically.

'Listen, why don't you light the fire, and could you rustle up a snack of some kind? I didn't stop for supper. Then I'll give you a hand packing the rest of this stuff.'

Tears pricked at her eyes. She got up and gave him a quick hug, snuggling into his shoulder affectionately. 'Jonathan, you're far too good for me,' she murmured. 'Of course I'll give you something to eat. And I'd really appreciate your help.'

'I have to fly to Charlottetown next week. There's the opening of a new exhibition at Confederation Centre and I'm invited to the reception. Maybe I can see you while I'm over there.'

'I'm sure by then I'll be delighted to see a face from home,' she answered cheerfully, and if this was not quite the response he had hoped for, he said nothing.

The rest of the evening passed very pleasantly, and it was only as Jonathan was leaving that he interjected a more serious note. Holding her by the shoulders, he said quietly, 'I wish you weren't quite so vulnerable, Anne—I'm very much afraid you'll get hurt all over again. If at any time you need me, will you promise to phone? If I'm not around, you can always leave a message with my answering service.'

'I promise—and thank you, Jonathan. I'll see you next week.'

CHAPTER THREE

Two days later Anne had her first glimpse of Stornaway, David's new home on the Island. She had crossed the Northumberland Strait on one of the big white-painted ferries, and had been met by a bright-eyed little man of sixty-odd, who introduced himself as Terence O'Connor and who apparently fulfilled the double function of chauffeur and handyman at Stornaway. He led her to a sleek black Mercedes—David's taste in cars had not changed, Anne thought wryly. She sat in the front seat be-. side Mr O'Connor, cushioned by the car's unobtrusive luxury. Now that she was nearly at her destination, she could feel the tension rising within her; luckily Terence O'Connor's favourite form of conversation appeared to be a monologue, so that all she had to do was provide an occasional remark. The car purred smoothly over the icy roads, and almost an hour passed before Mr O'Connor came to a halt on the edge of the road at the crest of a hill.

'You can see Stornaway from here,' he remarked. 'It's a right pretty sight—want to have a look?'

Glad of the chance to stretch her legs before her arrival, Anne climbed out of the car. It was late afternoon. The sun was sinking behind the gently rolling hills, tinting the sky and the snow a soft rose pink. The river that wound through the valley and emptied into the bay in front of her had a narrow channel, like a steel-grey ribbon, still unfrozen. Along the distant shoreline she could see a dark strip of the ocean, and then there was nothing but the whiteness of drift ice all the way to the horizon. The silence was absolute.

As though drawn by a magnet, her gaze fell to the house that lay below her—Stornaway. L-shaped, it nestled against the sloping hillside, protected from the ocean winds by a grove of tall spruce and naked-limbed maples. Its mullioned windows were reflecting the last rays of the sun; from its chimney rose a thin thread of blue smoke. Constructed of mellow ochre bricks and varnished cedar, it was as much a part of its environment as the hills and trees. Something about the house beckoned her irresistibly, tugging at her heart-strings, seeming to offer her a welcome ... a home. ... Angry that a mere house could affect her so greatly, she deliberately turned her back on the tranquil scene and went back to the car. David had always had impeccable taste and a sure eye for beauty and Stornaway was simply the expression of that taste. Any impression it might give of welcoming her was only a product of her imagination. She was arriving as an interloper, and she'd better remember that; she couldn't afford to get emotional over anything that belonged to David—except perhaps the child.

Her heartbeat quickened as they drove along the circular driveway and stopped in front of the huge oak door. On either side of it golden light splashed through the front windows on to the snow. She got out of the car, carrying her handbag and overnight case, Terence O'Connor following with the rest of her luggage. As she approached the house the door swung open, and for one panic-stricken moment she was convinced it would be David standing there. But no—it was an elderly grey-haired lady in a dark-hued dress.

'Welcome, Miss Winters, welcome. I'm Deirdre O'Connor. Come away in, dearie, it's too cold to be outdoors. Terence, take your boots off, now, before you track snow all over my carpets.'

Nervous as she was, Anne was amused to see the garrulous Terence meekly and promptly remove his footwear. She put down her case and unzipped her own knee-high leather boots, to a running commentary from Mrs O'Connor. 'I'm glad you're here. The wee girl needs company, and I'm too old to be out making snowmen and sliding down the hill. She misses her father when he's away, poor motherless little soul.'

Anne's heart skipped a beat. She had not expected to be presented with such a perfect opening so soon. Her face hidden as she removed her boots, she said with assumed casualness, 'What happened to her mother?'

'Upped and left as soon as the child was born—that's the story I heard. Heartless baggage! Mr Metcalfe won't have her name mentioned, that I do know.'

'I see,' said Anne, her soft mouth compressed. 'Story' was the right word. As naturally as she could, she added, 'I'm looking forward to meeting Jessica.'

'I'm sure she'll be down as soon as she realises you're here. In the meantime I'll show you to your room and then I have a nice dinner cooked for you. Terence, you'll carry up Miss Winters' bags.'

No wonder Terence talked so much when he was driving the car, Anne decided; he obviously didn't get the chance to say a word at home. She followed Mrs O'Connor down the hall, her stockinged feet sinking into the thick rug. As they went upstairs, she gained a confused impression of spacious, beautifully furnished rooms, of exquisite paintings and mgnificent carpets. Her own room overlooked the bay. The sun had set and the spruces stood black against the pale wintry sky while a single star twinkled in the heavens. Such beauty, Anne thought, for a minute almost forgetting her reason for being there.

Firmly Mrs O'Connor drew the curtains. 'It's a bleak place in winter,' she said matter-of-factly, blind to the lonely magnificence of the view. 'You'll not be wanting to look out on that. The bathroom's through this way, dear, and I'll serve your dinner in half an hour, how would that be? Jessica ate earlier, so you don't have to worry about her.'

'That would be lovely,' Anne murmured, feeling the tension twang at her overstretched nerves as the housekeeper left the room, softly closing the door behind her. It was a relief to be alone.

She looked around her. The curtains and bedspread were of a rich green velvet, the walls and carpeting a warm beige. A chair upholstered in patterned green brocade was on one side of the brick fireplace with a cherrywood desk and chair on the other. With a stab of pain she wondered if David had chosen the furnishings; their simple, un-cluttered lines were the sort of thing he would like.

She went into the bathroom to rinse her hands, the splash of water in the sink drowning out the opening and closing of the bedroom door. She dried herself on the luxuriously thick towel and carefully re-applied a pale pink lipstick that did absolutely nothing for her colouring. Then she brushed her hair back into a neat bun, thereby adding at least five years to her age. With the glasses perched on her nose she was satisfied that her appearance was about as far removed from the Anne of four years ago as it could be.

'Hello. I'm Jessica.'

Anne's comb clattered into the sink. Moving like an automaton, she turned around. A little girl was standing in the doorway, staring at her. She was wearing a green pina-fore dress and white tights. A plush teddy bear trailed from one hand.

'I—hello,' Anne croaked, wondering with a strange de-tachment if she was going to faint.

The child had David's tawny hair, although in her it was more a honey-gold; it curled in enchanting wisps around her ears. But her face was a miniature of Anne's: high cheekbones and long brows, eyes more green than grey, delicately pointed chin.

'You're Miss Winters, aren't you?' Jessica said solemnly.

'Yes—yes, I am,' said Anne, when with all her heart she longed to say, 'No—I'm your mother.' But she couldn't. She had begun this masquerade—now she had to carry it through. Dear God, she thought in speechless wonder, my child is alive! Jessica is mine. . . .

She knelt down, bringing her face to a level with Jessica's. 'Does your teddy have a name?'

'Pooh Bear,' said Jessica, with an air of explaining the obvious.

'Oh, of course. Then he must like honey.'

'I do too.'

Incredibly Anne found she could laugh in a natural and easy way. 'Do you both eat it for breakfast, or only for elevenses?'

'We have it on toast. But sometimes Dee-dee burns the toast. I don't like the black bits.'

The child's grimace made Anne chuckle with delight; Dee-dee must be Deirdre O'Connor. 'We're going to be great friends,' she said confidently. 'I can tell.'

'Will you read me a story before I go to bed? Daddy always does when he's home.'

Anne's eyelashes flickered down. 'Of course I will,' she said, while inwardly castigating herself; she must learn not to react every time David's name was mentioned. 'Do you think you could show me the way to the kitchen? Mrs O'Connor has dinner ready for me.'

Together they went downstairs, Pooh Bear bumping on each step just like his namesake. For Anne the evening was one of pure delight. Her dinner was served in what Mrs O'Connor called the alcove, a small room off the kitchen with sunshine-yellow flowered wallpaper, white wicker furniture, and graceful ivy plants hanging by the windows. As Anne ate the piping hot meat pie followed by a creamy chocolate soufflé, Jessica chattered away about her new sled, the doings of Pooh Bear, and her longing for a pair of skates. 'Daddy said he might bring them back with him. I hope he does.' Wistfully she glanced over at Anne, who felt her very bones melt with love.

After supper Jessica took Anne on a somewhat haphazard tour of the house, starting with the back porch. This was not by chance, Anne decided, looking around at the neatly arranged skiing equipment, toboggans, and snowsuits.

'We could play in the snow tomorrow,' Anne said hopefully.

'P'rhaps. I like skiing with Daddy best,' was the not very enthusiastic response—the first inkling for Anne that there might be difficulties ahead.

Jessica's own room was next, a charming little girl's room decorated in pastel shades, next to Anne's room. What seemed to Anne an over-abundance of expensive toys was tidily arranged on the shelves; she was more pleased to see the variety of books neatly lined up beside the toys. Then the child led her down to the end of the hall and pushed open a door. 'This is Daddy's room,' she announced, and it would not have needed much discernment to sense the loneliness behind the words. Anne felt a spurt of anger against the man who could leave his daughter in the care of a woman he had never met. But this was lost in the welter of other emotions as she silently gazed around her at her ex-husband David's bedroom.

A large room with the wall that overlooked the ocean was nothing but a great sheet of glass. Curtains of midnight blue and walls were a cold uncompromising grey. The vast bed—her eyes flinched away from it—was also covered in midnight blue. A pure white carpet. A grey stone fireplace. The only note of colour in the room came from the laden bookshelves. It was an austere room, intensely masculine; it spoke of coldness and control.

She jumped when Jessica spoke. 'Will you read me a story now?'

'Oh, sure.'

After Jessica's bath there came a snack of cookies and milk, the mandatory bedtime story, and prayers, her 'God bless Daddy' catching in Anne's throat. She longed to kiss her daughter goodnight, but knew she could not rush the child, for Jessica would not have felt any of the instinctive flood of love that had so disarmed Anne. So she contented herself with a 'Goodnight, dear. I'm just down the hall if you need anything,' as she left the room.

For a long time she sat quietly by the window in her own room. Staring unseeingly out over the bay, she relived every minute of her brief acquaintance with her daughter, filled again with the wonder that so beautiful a child could be hers. Then she thought again of the severity and asceticism of David's bedroom; in that room slept the man who four years ago had brutally lied to her. He had told her that her baby was dead and that he did not want to see her ever again, discarding her with as little feeling as if she was a worn-out garment ... he had deprived her of Jessica, child of her own body, flesh of her flesh.... Anne clenched her hands in her lap, overwhelmed by a tumult of passionate hatred. Somehow she would get her revenge, no matter how long she had to wait.

The next day was a day of discovery for Anne, for it was her first full day in Jessica's company. She had slept deeply, which was contrary to her usual habit in a strange place. It was as though Stornaway felt like home simply because of Jessica's presence. Jessica ... her daughter.

She lay quietly in bed, thinking of the day ahead with anticipation. Already she knew certain things about Jessica: her loneliness for her father, her lack of shyness with Anne, her good manners that were coupled with a degree of self-possession surprising in one so young. Probably that had sprung from being left alone a good deal, Anne thought with a rush of protective love. Now Jessica need be alone no longer.

Although the child had been friendly enough, Anne was sure it would take time to win her trust and affection, and that was time Anne was well prepared to spend. Since David was apparently not due back for two weeks, she could look forward to several uninterrupted days with Jessica, a prospect that entranced her.

When she went downstairs, Jessica was already seated at the table in the alcove, eating a bowl of porridge liberally sprinkled with brown sugar. Deirdre presented Anne with a similar bowlful and Anne went to join her daughter.

'Good morning, Jessica,' she said, an irrepressible lilt in her voice. Even the weather matched her mood, for the sun was pouring in through the long windows, while outside the snow lay blindingly bright on the hills. She saw now that the alcove had been constructed in such a fashion as to obtain the best view of the countryside. Childishly she longed to get outside and explore.

'Hi, Miss Winters,' Jessica responded gravely.

Anne was concerned to see how pale the child looked. 'Let's go outside after breakfast,' she suggested. 'Okay?'

Jessica poked at her porridge. 'I usually only play outdoors with Daddy.'

Feeling her way carefully over what she sensed was dangerous ground, Anne said gently, 'Oh, why is that?'

'Dee-dee doesn't like to go out. And there's no one else to play with. When Daddy's home, he takes me skiing and tobogganing.' Her lower lip quivered. 'I wish he was here.'

Fighting down fury that David would put business interests ahead of his daughter's welfare, Anne said quietly, 'You must miss him a lot.'

Jessica nodded, holding Pooh Bear a little closer with her free arm.

'Aren't there any other children around?'

'There's the Haleys—they have three boys. But I'm not allowed to go there by myself, it's too far.'

'Well, I'm sure I can take you there, if you'd like to go. So what do you do to amuse yourself when your father's away?'

'I watch television and play in my room. Sometimes Dee-dee lets me help her make cookies.'

Anne drew a deep breath, knowing she could not allow any of the hostility she was feeling towards David to colour her voice. 'I really like being outdoors, Jessica. Would you feel like doing me a favour this morning?'

'I guess so,' the child said warily.

'Would you take me on a bit of a tour outside? Perhaps you could show me where you use your new sled.'

'All right.'

'Good!' Deliberately Anne changed the subject, feeling as though she had won a major victory. 'Would you like a piece of toast?'

After breakfast they both got dressed in snowsuits, Anne lending a hand with the zippers on Jessica's boots. They took the sled with them, Jessica dragging it behind her as she pointed out the wing on the house where the O'Connor's lived, and the shed where all the garden tools were

kept. 'Daddy said I could have my own garden this summer. I'm going to grow pumpkins for Hallowe'en and lots
of radishes—I think they're a pretty colour.'

'Carrots are fun to grow too, and they taste so good
when you eat them right out of the garden,' Anne remarked,
noticing how often the words 'Daddy says' were part of
Jessica's conversation. In their wanderings they had come
to the slope behind the house, so Anne showed Jessica
how to stand up on the sled, steering with the ropes. This
obviously intrigued the child and she went up and down
the slope trying to master the new technique, shrieking
with laughter when she fell into the snow. It was nearly
noon when Anne noticed the first signs of tiring; she said
quickly, 'Let's go home now and see what's for lunch. I'm
starving!'

When they sat down to eat, she was pleased to see colour
in Jessica's cheeks, and doubly pleased to sense the beginnings of real friendliness in the little girl's manner.

As the days passed each other, the companionship
deepened between them. Because 'Marianne' was too much
of a mouthful for Jessica, the diminutive 'Anne' was decided upon instead, an arrangement that naturally suited
Anne; the sound of the childish voice calling her name
filled her with joy. Jessica would tuck her mittened hand
confidently in Anne's now, as they walked up the lane to
get the mail; she trusted her with the little confidences of
a four-year-old: her fear of snakes and spiders, her longing
for a puppy. 'Daddy says I'm too young to look after one
yet and he's away too much. Maybe next year....' Then
came the night when, after her bedtime prayers, Jessica
wrapped her arms around Anne's neck and said sleepily, 'I
love you, Anne. I'm glad you came. Will you stay for ever
and for ever?'

'Oh darling, I love you too,' Anne said softly, feeling the
tears crowd her eyes, her cheek pressed against Jessica's
curly head. Then she felt the child stiffen in her arms.
'What's wrong?'

'Daddy, Daddy!' Jessica tore herself free of Anne and

ran across the room to be gathered into the arms of the tall
man standing silently in the doorway.

Anne stayed where she was, seated on the bed. Indeed
she was not sure whether her legs would have supported
her. The moment she had subconsciously been dreading
for years was upon her: she was face to face with David.
Her palms were suddenly slippery with sweat and at the
base of her throat a pulse beat frantically.

She had a moment's respite as David hugged his daughter, and it gave her time to give thanks she was wearing a
plain grey dress, her hair in a severe chignon, her face
innocent of make-up. Fortunately for her peace of mind,
she was unaware of the unconscious pride in her bearing,
of the slender length of her legs with their fine-boned
ankles and feet.

'You didn't tell me you were coming, Daddy!' Jessica
reproached him.

'I didn't know until the last minute, sweetheart.'

'It was a surprise!' she crowed.

'Mmm, that's right.' He paused, his blue eyes penetrating as he gazed at the still figure on the bed. 'Maybe you'd
better introduce me to this lady, Jessica?'

'It's Anne,' his daughter replied with devastating simplicity.

Anne winced. 'My name is Marianne Winters, Mr Metcalfe,' she said coolly. 'But Jessica had trouble with the
Marianne, so we thought Anne would be simpler.' Wanting
to deflect the conversation, she added, 'I do hope you don't
object to us being on a first name basis? Miss Winters
seems such a mouthful.'

'Not at all. And Anne is a delightful name.'

There was a charged silence. Anne moistened her lips,
desperately trying to think of something to say. But
Jessica forestalled her. 'She's lots of fun, Daddy. Can she
stay? I don't want her to go away!'

It was not the first time that Anne had noticed Jessica's
deep craving for security. Her eyes darkened to a smoky
grey, anger giving her added strength for the difficulties she

foresaw ahead of her. David Metcalfe walked closer to the bed, stopping only a couple of feet away from her. Because he was towering over her, she got to her feet, uncoiling the slim length of her legs in a graceful movement. She noticed that in flat heels she barely reached his chin.

His face was an inscrutable mask, his eyes hard as ice. 'Strange,' he said slowly, 'you remind me of someone I used to know.'

She tilted her chin defiantly. 'Really? Who was that?'

'Oh, no one important.'

Unconsciously her eyes flashed fire even as she said with complete untruth, 'As far as I'm aware, Mr Metcalfe, I've never seen you before in my life.'

He raised a disdainful eyebrow. 'I wasn't suggesting that you were that person, Miss—er—Winters, only that you reminded me of her.'

Hot colour suffused Anne's cheeks, but luckily before she could say anything, Jessica again intervened. 'Can I stay up a bit later tonight, Daddy?' she coaxed. 'Please?'

He glanced down at the little girl, his features softening. He seized her in both hands, swinging her high in the air until she shrieked with excitement. Feeling very much left out, Anne watched in silence. Whatever faults he might have, there could be no doubt that David loved his daughter. She felt suddenly very tired. 'If you'll excuse me,' she murmured, 'I think I'll go to my room.'

David glanced at his watch. 'By all means,' he said. 'But perhaps you'll join me in the study for cocktails in—let's say an hour?'

However politely it was worded, it was an order, not a request. 'I'd really rather not——' she began.

'Come, Miss Winters, I'm sure you can find time for us to have a little chat. I promise not to keep you from your beauty sleep.' He glanced derisively at her unbecoming dress and severe hairstyle.

'Very well,' she said stiffly. Wanting only to escape, she gave Jessica a quick kiss on the cheek. 'See you tomorrow, poppet.'

'Night, Anne.' As though she had sensed the strain between the adults, Jessica added anxiously, 'Aren't you glad
my daddy's home?'

'Of course I am.' Avoiding David's sardonic gaze, she
hastily left the room.

Closing the door of her own room, she leaned against
the panels; she was shaking uncontrollably and wanted
nothing more than to fling herself on the bed and cry her
eyes out. But she could not allow herself that luxury, for in
an hour she had to meet David again, this time without
Jessica's presence to act as a buffer. She would need all her
wits about her. For in Jessica's bedroom he had been playing with her, as a cat plays with a mouse. In spite of her
changed appearance and her new identity, had he recognised her? The prospect was terrifying and she could feel
herself sliding into a mindless panic. Her elegant and
luxurious room suddenly seemed like a cage. Impulsively
she grabbed her coat and gloves and after a swift glance
down the hall to make sure neither David nor Jessica was
in sight, sped down the stairs. After pulling on her boots at
the back door, she stepped outside.

It was dark and bitterly cold, the raw north wind whip-
ping her cheeks. Turning her back on it, she hurried up
the hill, her hands thrust deep in her pockets. Her footsteps
crunched in the snow. It was too cold for coherent thought;
all her energies were concentrated on moving fast enough
to keep warm, and on protecting her exposed skin from the
wind's icy fingers.

She was only gone for about half an hour. But as she
ran back up the stairs to her room, she knew she had done
the right thing. The moment of paralysing fear was gone.
She was simply allowing her imagination to run away with
her by thinking that David had recognised her. To him she
was Marianne Winters, a prim and proper young woman
who was Jessica's new companion.

As she applied powder to her red cheeks, she mentally
rehearsed everything the real Marianne had told her about
life in Fredericton, until she was sure she had it at the tip

of her tongue. Then she put on the tinted pair of glasses she
had bought in Halifax; their lenses had a greyish tinge in
electric light, and made a quite astonishing difference to her
appearance. A demure pearl brooch on her collar, the bland
pink lipstick on her mouth, and she was ready. The cool
and correct Miss Marianne Winters would now make polite
conversation with her new employer....

Unfortunately it did not quite turn out that way,
although it started off smoothly enough. Anne had not been
in the study before, since she had gathered it was more or
less off limits when David was away. David was not yet
there, so while she waited she looked around her appreciatively. The room was panelled in pale and gleaming pine
boards, decorated with some attractive military prints. A
fireplace of beach stones took up most of the west wall
while bookshelves lined the opposite wall. A magnificent
set of stereophonic equipment, some deep and comfortable
armchairs and a chesterfield comprised the rest of the furnishings, along with a businesslike oak desk. There was a
warmth and sense of relaxation about this room that had
been lacking in David's bedroom; it looked more like the
old David she had known years ago, the David who had
swept her off her feet and made passionate love to her....

'You look very pensive.'

She jumped. Whirling to face him, she prayed that her
thoughts had not been reflected in her face.

'What were you thinking about?'

'I—I was admiring this room,' she prevaricated. 'It's very
attractive.'

'What can I pour you?' From the mockery in his voice
she knew he was not convinced by her explanation.

'A sherry would be fine—dry, preferably.' This was a
newly acquired taste; the young Anne had preferred exotic
cocktails, the more colourful and laden with fruit, the
better.

He came over to her, holding out a long-stemmed glass,
his eyes trained on hers. As she took it from him, their
fingers touched and it took every ounce of her control to
keep her gaze calm and steady on his.

She had made a devastating discovery when his hand brushed hers. That feather-light touch had ripped through every nerve in her body, in an instant awakening her long-dormant flesh. She tingled with awareness, remembering with frightening clarity long-forgotten details of their love-making. She would be as helpless to resist him now as she had always been. She hated him ... yet she desired him with equal intensity. He must never guess—never. For she would be lost if he did. Casually moving away from him, she thanked him for the drink.

David knelt by the fireplace and put a match to the heaped papers and logs. As he crouched there, his attention on the fire, she studied him unobtrusively.

He had changed in four years. There were new lines carved in his cheeks and in repose his mouth was severe. The blue eyes gave nothing away. It was not a happy face; there was about it an unmistakable air of disillusion. But as he stood up she became fully aware of what had not changed. His height for one thing. The lean line of his hips and thighs, the muscular breadth of his shoulders. He carried with him an aura of intense masculinity, all the more powerful for being more or less unstudied; it was as much a part of him as the tawny head of hair, the long shapely fingers, and the formidable intelligence. Again she felt that treacherous weakening of her body and the pull of desire.

'Have I got egg on my chin?' he said irritably.

She had the grace to blush. 'Have you lived here long, Mr Metcalfe?' she said at random.

'Less than a year. And you—you're from Fredericton, aren't you?'

'Yes, I was born there, and I worked there the last two years, at the day centre on College Road,' she answered glibly.

'Why did you leave?'

She fiddled with her glass. 'I felt I needed a change.'

'That's fortunate for us,' he said smoothly. 'Jessica seems to have taken quite a fancy to you. I would gather it's mutual?'

She glanced over at him—his body had the tautness of a

lion about to pounce. For whatever reason, he was deliberately baiting her, she thought grimly. Well, two could play that game. 'Yes, it is,' she said calmly. 'She's a dear little girl. It's a pity she should feel so insecure.'

His eyes narrowed. 'Perhaps you wouldn't mind explaining yourself? I was under the impression that I'd hired a nurse, not a psychologist.'

'One doesn't need to be a psychologist to sense Jessica's insecurity,' she said crisply. 'She misses you when you're away. And she seems preoccupied with the notion that I too might go away.' Recklessly she threw down the gauntlet. 'I would presume it springs from her lack of a mother.'

He drew in his breath with a vicious hiss. 'Let's get something straight right now, Miss Winters. Jessica's mother is my business, not yours. Is that perfectly clear?'

His eyes bored into hers and unconsciously she shrank back into her chair, for the first time sensing the violence in him, now barely held in check. 'I'm sorry,' she stammered. 'I shouldn't have said that.'

'No, you shouldn't,' he agreed unpleasantly.

She drew herself up with a certain dignity. 'Nevertheless, she does miss you when you're gone. When I first came, I discovered that she scarcely played outdoors at all while you were away, preferring to watch television and stay in her room. That hardly seems healthy in a four-year-old. Particularly when you're not home for two or three weeks at a time.' There was an undeniable air of accusation in her level gaze.

'My absences are for business reasons and hence unavoidable. That's the reason I hired you, Miss Winters, to be company for her while I'm gone. Kindly restrict yourself to doing just that—and refrain from theorising about her upbringing.'

'Yes, sir!' she snapped, her temper getting the better of her, although she quailed inwardly as he got up. Without asking her permission, he removed her glass from her nerveless fingers and refilled it with the pale golden liquid, pouring himself another highball at the same time. A warning bell sounded in Anne's brain; she had a notoriously weak head for alcohol.

'You know, Miss Winters,' he said silkily, 'you present some rather interesting contrasts. You sit there prim as a nun in your grey dress—and I'm sure you're woman enough to realise just how unbecoming it is—with your hair scraped back and your nose shining. Portrait of a Victorian miss. Yet I'd be willing to swear that under that correct and proper exterior of yours there breathes fire and passion. There's certainly a temper!'

'Quite possibly a lot of Victorian misses were outwardly deceptive,' she replied unwisely. 'It was their subjugation in a male-dominated society that forced them into passive roles. Or primness, if you prefer that word.'

'Ah, and are you using the same excuse?'

'What do you mean?' she asked weakly. Damn—how had she got into this? He was steering the conversation into the channels he desired and helplessly she had to follow in his wake.

'Is your life dominated by some male?'

'No! This is the twentieth century, not the nineteenth.'

'But you are, to use your phrase, "outwardly deceptive". Just why are you dressed in that manner, Miss Winters?'

'It was not explained to me when I took the job that I had to dress to please my employer,' she retorted.

To her amazement, David threw back his head and laughed. 'Touché!'

He had always been irresistible in laughter. In spite of herself Anne felt a smile tug at her lips.

'You realise, by the way, that you've just proved my point,' he went on. 'The correct Miss Winters would never be rude to her employer.'

'Then her employer shouldn't be rude to her!'

'Take your glasses off.'

She gasped with shock. She had begun to enjoy this repartee—and now this. Putting all the conviction in her tone of which she was capable, she answered, 'I can't—I'm as blind as a bat without them.'

'Are you?' Again she knew he did not believe her. 'That's a pity. It must be inconvenient at times.'

'Not really, I've learned to live with it.' She took another sip of sherry, feeling it slide smoothly down her throat.

'It's surprising what one can learn to live with, isn't it?'

'I—I don't know what you mean,' she stammered. The strain of their conversation was beginning to tell on her; she could feel the beginnings of a headache throbbing in her temples.

'Don't tell me you're too young never to have been let down by another person—never to have known the inevitable transcience of love?'

The alcohol eroded her caution. For one mad moment she contemplated telling him the truth, of just how bitterly he himself had disillusioned her four years ago; she could feel her anger burgeoning within her at the memory of his cruelty. But then the image of Jessica's little face appeared before her—her relationship with Jessica was too new, too precariously balanced for her to risk destroying it. So she said sarcastically, 'I'm afraid not, Mr Metcalfe. I'm perhaps less experienced in these matters than you.'

'Experience can always be gained, Miss Winters.'

Abruptly she stood up, totally unnerved by the implicit threat in his words. 'Please will you excuse me? I'm tired,' she said. It was the truth—she had had enough.

'Scared, Miss Winters?' he taunted.

'Should I be?'

'I think perhaps you should.'

Oh God, she had to get out of here. 'Goodnight,' she gasped.

'Sleep well, my dear. I'll see you tomorrow.' There was no mistaking the threat in his voice now.

Forgetting her dignity, Anne fled from the room. Upstairs in her bedroom she undressed with trembling haste, viciously pulling the pins from her hair and brushing it loose. The headache had become a pounding reality and as she swallowed a couple of aspirins she stared at herself in the mirror—huge grey eyes in a pinched face. She had been a fool to even try matching wits with David. Did he know who she really was? Or had he changed so much that he had to ridicule and belittle every female he came across? She had no way of knowing. . . .

Contrary to his last mocking remark, she did not sleep well; she spent a good part of the night staring up into the blackness. As can so easily happen in the small hours of the morning, she completely lost her sense of proportion, and the nightmare conviction that David knew exactly who she was, and was just waiting for the best opportunity to expose her, dominated her thoughts. Finally she sank into a sleep of utter exhaustion.

A light tap on the door awakened her. 'Yes?' she murmured drowsily.

Deirdre O'Connor poked her neat grey head around the door. 'I've brought you your breakfast, dearie,' she said, entering the room with a tray.

Confused, Anne said, 'Why, how lovely! But am I late or something?'

'It's past ten, but there's no harm done. Mr Metcalfe and the wee girl have gone to Charlottetown together. He said not to disturb you, you needed your beauty sleep.' There was a wealth of speculation in the housekeeper's eyes.

Anne could feel colour creeping into her cheeks. 'This is very kind of you,' she said firmly. 'Did they say when they'd be back?'

'After lunch, I believe. So just take your time, dearie.'

Thoughtfully Anne began to eat. Damn the man—beauty sleep indeed! He'd know Mrs O'Connor well enough to be certain the remark would get back to Anne.

So they had gone to Charlottetown, the two of them. She, Miss Winters, had not been invited. After all, why should she be? As a paid companion, she would undoubtedly appreciate a morning off. However, the situation was far different, of course, and Anne was aware of a bewildering mêlée of jealousy and loneliness as she thought of father and daughter leaving her behind; they would enjoy themselves without her, there was no doubt of that. But she was Jessica's mother—she should be with her. Ridiculously she felt like crying. For the first time since she had come here she remembered how Marianne and Jonathan had both tried to warn her how easily she could be hurt should she go to the Island. It began to look as though they were right.

The afternoon was to dispel some of these fears. Anne was curled up in an armchair in the study, reading, when she heard the car come back. Within minutes Jessica burst into the room, followed more slowly by David. He looked disturbingly handsome in a camelhair wool overcoat over a tailored dark brown business suit.

'Oh, Anne!' the little girl cried. 'Daddy's going to take me tobogganing. Will you come too?'

Anne's eyes flew to David, but he gave her no clue as to his feelings. 'I don't know. . . .'

'Please come! It'll be fun.' Jessica was wearing a cherry-red coat with a white fur hat and mittens, and her little face was alight with anticipation. Anne was helpless to resist her.

'All right, I'll come. I guess we'd better get changed.'

So far David had not said a word, but as she walked past him to go upstairs he said softly, too softly for Jessica to hear, 'Did you sleep well, Miss Winters?'

Behind her glasses, her eyes flashed fire. 'Not particularly, no.'

'Guilty conscience?'

Suddenly she was tired of his verbal fencing. 'I don't think *I'm* the one who should have a guilty conscience!'

His body grew taut; he looked as sleek and dangerous as a jungle cat. 'That I find debatable.'

'Hurry up, Anne!' Jessica called impatiently from the stairs, and gladly Anne made her escape.

Once they all got outside, it was as though there was a temporary truce. It was a bright, windless day, the temperature just below freezing. The sky was an incredibly deep blue—as blue as David's eyes, Anne found herself thinking unwillingly—and the snow a dazzling white, crisp and fluffy underfoot. Black as pitch a pair of crows flew overhead, their raucous cries diminishing in the distance. Anne took a deep breath of the clean cold air, feeling tinglingly alive.

They walked past the house to the crest of a hill. Its slope was gradual at first, then steepened alarmingly before ending in a level field. 'You don't mean we're going down that?' Anne squawked in exaggerated dismay.

Jessica plunked herself at the front of the toboggan. 'You next, Anne,' she ordered. 'Hold on tight!'

Anne did as she was told, tucking her legs around Jessica's body. Then she felt David sit behind her, his hands firm on her waist. One part of her longed to lean back against him, to be encircled in the protective curve of his arms, even as her other self jeered at such foolishness. David pushed off. Slowly at first, then gathering momentum, the toboggan sped down the hill. The wind whipped Anne's cheeks. Jessica shrieked with delight as they hit a bump, flew in the air and landed with a thud on the hard-pressed snow. They finally came to a halt a scant ten feet from the fence. Breathless and exhilarated, they scrambled to their feet.

They must have done this half a dozen times—racing down the hill, trudging back up again, taking turns to pull the toboggan. Their laughter rang out over the hillside. The exercise and the excitement engendered a sense of camaraderie and more than once Anne was visited by the thought that this was what a family was like—father, mother and child, having fun together. Strangely the thought gave her joy rather than pain, for David was so relaxed and cheerful a companion that the tension between them had disappeared as though it had never been.

'Last time,' he said firmly, ignoring Jessica's cries of dismay. 'I'm too old for these shenanigans.'

Outlined against the blue sky, the sun glinting on his fair hair, he looked so vivid and alive that Anne's breath caught in her throat. She suddenly became aware that he was staring at her equally hard. She had forgotten how un-

like the prim Miss Winters she must look. Her two-piece
snowsuit, which she had had for over a year, was a vivid
green; she had tucked her hair under a tasselled green and
white cap, but wisps of it had escaped; her cheeks glowed
with colour. The fashionably shaped dark glasses gave her
an air of mystery and aloofness belied by the delightful
smile on her lips.

'Two more turns, Daddy!' Jessica pleaded.

'Nope—last time.'

He shoved off and unconsciously Anne leaned into the
curve of his arms. But this time when the toboggan hit the
bump, it landed at an angle, and all three of them tumbled
into a snowbank. Jessica emerged first, her eyebrows and
hat frosted with snow crystals. 'Hey, Daddy,' she chuckled,
'you're squashing Anne!'

Anne was lying on her back in the snow. Somehow David
had landed on top of her, his weight crushing her, his face
a scant few inches from hers. 'Are you okay?' he demanded.

All her defences down, she began to laugh. 'There's ice
melting down my neck!' she wailed.

Twin devils of mischief dancing in his eyes, he seized a
handful of snow and let it fall from his fingers on her
flushed face. She wriggled helplessly, pinioned by his
weight.

'You're mean, Daddy,' Jessica chortled.

David glanced over at his daughter. 'Who, me?' he said
innocently.

It gave Anne the chance she needed. She worked one
arm free, and before David could duck she shoved some of
the icy crystals down the neck of his parka.

'You'll pay for that!' he grinned. Getting to his feet, he
swung her up in his arms. 'Where'll we put her, Jess?'

'In the snowbank, in the snowbank!'

Anne beat ineffectively at his chest with her mittened
fists. 'Put me down, you brute!' she cried.

'Oh? If you insist——' and he dropped her unceremoniously in the heaped up snow.

Laughing so hard she could feel the tears rolling down

her cheeks, she looked up at them both—Jessica, chubby in her red snowsuit, her little teeth gleaming like pearls, David, standing over her with legs straddled, vibrant and totally male. Everything distilled into a moment of pure happiness that left her shaken by its intensity.

David reached out a hand and pulled her to her feet, his gloved hands brushing the snow from her face and jacket. 'Why don't you get the toboggan, Jessica?' he suggested casually. As the little girl went out of earshot, he said quietly, 'I begin to see infinite possibilities in you, Miss Winters.' Before she could move, he tweaked the cap from her head. Her hair tumbled loose about her shoulders, shining like heavy silk. He picked up a strand. 'Beautiful hair. You will oblige me by not wearing it scraped back any more in that dreadful bun.'

Mesmerised by the brilliance of his eyes, she could think of nothing to say. As Jessica returned with the toboggan, the three of them headed back to the house.

Although she and David never quite regained the closeness they had experienced on the hillside, the rest of the day passed pleasantly enough. David made no more barbed remarks. When Anne went to bed she felt reassured, certain that she was accepted at face value as Marianne Winters. Perhaps she had carried it a bit far, dressing in so unbecoming a fashion; it seemed as though that had made him suspicious. She could probably afford to relax and bring out one or two of her more colourful outfits. It was a great relief to know that she was safe and he had not connected her with his estranged wife, and she had no trouble falling asleep that night.

CHAPTER FOUR

SHORTLY after midnight something woke her. She found herself sitting bolt upright in bed, her ears straining at the silence. There it was again—a sharp piercing cry in the dark. It was coming from Jessica's room.

Reaching for her brown velour robe, she pulled it around her as she ran down the hall. She switched on the bedside lamp so that a soft yellow glow illuminated the room. Jessica was tossing in her sleep, whimpering under her breath.

'Wake up, pet,' Anne whispered, gathering the little girl into her arms.

Jessica's eyes flew open, dark with panic. Her face crumpled and she buried her curly head in Anne's breast, beginning to cry. 'There was a snake,' she sobbed, 'he was chasing me.'

Rocking her back and forth, Anne held the child close until she had quietened. Fortunately the pocket of her robe yielded a handkerchief. 'Blow,' she ordered, and Jessica obediently raised a tear-blotched face. 'There, that's better, isn't it? It was a dream, dear, a bad dream.'

'Mmm—I was scared,' Jessica hiccupped.

'Snuggle under the covers before you get cold and I'll tell you a story,' Anne offered.

Jessica's eyes brightened. 'Make one up about Pooh Bear,' she said, hugging her teddy with one arm while her other hand stayed tightly clasped in Anne's.

'Once upon a time, far away in the Big Forest....' Anne began, making her voice as soothing as possible. Before long Jessica's eyes drooped shut and her breathing grew regular. Anne stopped talking, loosening her fingers from Jessica's hold. For a few minutes she remained there, all the love she felt for her little daughter in her face. Then she sighed, straightening her cramped limbs. She'd better go back to bed or she would never be able to get up in the morning.

After flipping off the bedside light she stood still, waiting for her eyes to adjust to the dark. To her surprise there seemed to be a dim light in the hallway. Puzzled, she walked through Jessica's door and straight into the arms of the man standing there. She gave a gasp of fright. 'Oh, David, how you scared me!' she stammered, not even noticing how naturally she had called him by his first name. Wide-eyed with shock, she instinctively raised both hands to his chest to push herself away from him.

Time stood still. Her palms were flat against the tangled mat of hair on his chest, for he was naked to the waist; the warmth of his skin scorched her flesh. His hands were firm on her hips, and his face so close to hers that she could feel his breath fanning her cheek. Over four years had passed since he had made love to her; temporarily the long months with all their pain and disillusion evaporated, leaving her with only a burning desire to lose herself in the hardness of his body, to reach the peaks of pleasure she had so often attained with him.

It was he who spoke first. 'I'm sorry I frightened you. Didn't you see me?'

'No, I didn't.'

'You wouldn't, of course——'

'Oh?'

'You're not wearing your glasses.'

Frantically she tried to recover her wits. 'I heard Jessica crying, so I didn't take the time to put them on.'

'I see. You look much better without them.'

She backed away. The even quality of David's voice was in itself a subtle menace. With a studied insolence he ran his eyes up and down her slender form. The velour robe clung to the curves of her figure. At its deep neckline could be seen the lace edging of her nightgown and the shadowed valley between her breasts. Her vulnerable mouth, clouded grey eyes, and dark-winged brows—leisurely he surveyed them all. 'More and more interesting, Miss Winters,' he drawled. 'You'll be pleased to know that your camouflage has been most effective. I had no idea you were hiding such —er—delectable charms.'

'Oh, stop talking like some eighteenth-century Don Juan!' she snapped, too much on edge to be tactful.

'You prefer action to talk?' He reached her in one swift stride, seizing her by the shoulders. Anne shrank back, making a tiny whimper of protest, but he ignored it. With bruising strength he fastened his mouth on hers. Summoning every ounce of her willpower, she remained rigid in his grasp, her lips cold and unresponsive under his.

Roughly he pushed her away, his eyes brilliant with anger. 'Don't think you've fooled me,' he grated. 'You're no frigid little miss!'

She flung at him the only weapon she had. 'Are you trying to force me to leave, Mr Metcalfe? Is that what you want?'

'It was David a minute ago,' he said unpleasantly. 'And the answer is no. Jessica likes you, and that's all, I'm interested in. I was merely trying to alert you to the dangers of presenting yourself as other than you are.'

Another of his damned double entendres. 'It would seem the safest course of action with you around,' she said spitefully.

'Don't flatter yourself that I have designs on your virtue.'

'You could have fooled me—or do you kiss everyone like that?'

Before she could guess his intention, he slid his arms around her with a gentleness that did not hide the hint of steel. 'Sometimes I kiss like this,' he said softly. With one hand he smoothed the hair back from her brow and traced the line of her cheek to her mouth, his blue eyes holding her hypnotised. He tilted her chin and then his lips brushed against hers, softly, almost tenderly, back and forth, teasing them open. His touch became firmer, more demanding, as he drank of the sweetness of her mouth.

All her resistance fled. As ice melts in the sun, her rigid

body softened and grew pliant in his arms. Her hands slid about his waist, her fingers probing the taut muscles of his back. Her lips parted under his. Her body moulded itself against him, the fullness of her breasts crushed to the hardness of his chest. It had been so long ... too long. ...

Lost in a gathering tumult of desire, she was too shocked to make a sound when he thrust her away from him in one brutally swift movement. Her back thudded against the wall. 'You little bitch!' he sneered. 'You're no different from the rest, are you?'

It was too much. 'I hate you,' she whispered brokenly, knowing it for the absolute truth. It gave her a glorious sense of freedom to be able to tell him at least that much of the truth. 'I hate you!' she spat again, her voice rising.

'Be quiet,' he said coldly, in perfect control of himself. 'Do you want to waken Jessica?'

Ashamed that she could have forgotten the proximity of the child's room, Anne lowered her voice. 'If you touch me again,' she hissed, 'I shall leave—do you understand?'

'I understand perfectly. It's called blackmail.'

Her palm itched to strike him, and something of her intention must have shown on her face. 'Don't do it,' David warned, 'you'll come off the worse in that as well. I think it's time we called a halt to this charming little scene, Miss Winters—or may I call you Marianne?' He gave her a mocking salute, although his eyes were granite-hard. 'Goodnight.' Pivoting, he walked away from her. His door closed and she was left in total darkness. Her hands groping along the wall, she made her way to her own room, where she pulled off her robe and huddled under the blankets; her feet were cold and her knees wouldn't stop trembling. It was a long time before she slept.

Although she dreaded meeting David the next morning, she was granted an unexpected reprieve. Jessica knocked on her door just as she finished dressing. 'Are you up, Anne?'

'Yes, come in, dear. How are you this morning?'

Still wearing her pyjamas, Jessica trailed into the room.

'Daddy's got to go away again,' she pouted.

Anne was sorry for Jessica, but couldn't help feeling a lightening of her own mood. 'How long will he be gone?'

'Don't know. He wants to see you before he goes, he said.'

'Oh.' For a moment Anne's hands grew still, then she resumed brushing her hair. Leaving it loose on her shoulders, she made a last-minute adjustment to her tweed skirt. 'Let's go and see him, and then we'll have breakfast. Remember I promised you a new colouring book? Perhaps we could walk to the store this morning and get one.'

The little girl brightened. 'Okay. New crayons too?'

'We'll see,' Anne laughed.

Hand in hand they descended the wide staircase. David's leather suitcase stood in the hall; he came out of the study, pulling on his gloves, just as they reached the bottom step.

'Hi, Jess. Good morning, Miss Winters,' he said formally. 'Did I mention last night that I had to be away for a couple of days? Just a local trip, it shouldn't take too long.'

'No, you didn't mention that,' she said drily, her eyes flinging back his challenge.

'I'll be passing through Fredericton—is there anyone you'd like me to get in touch with?'

'No, thank you,' she murmured, her mouth suddenly dry.

'When will you be back, Daddy?'

He knelt to hug Jessica. The two fair heads so close to each other brought a lump in Anne's throat. 'Saturday afternoon at the latest, sweetheart. Be a good girl while I'm gone, won't you?'

Terence O'Connor opened the front door. 'Car's set to go, sir. Any time you're ready.'

David kissed his daughter, gave Anne a cool nod, and went out, closing the door behind him. Jessica ran to the window to wave goodbye. And that was that, Anne thought. At least she could relax for a day or two. But even as she thought this, a worried frown creased her forehead. Why should David be going to Fredericton? Surely not to check on Miss Marianne Winters.... Her lips compressed.

'Are you sad Daddy's gone away?' Jessica asked.

'No, dear, I was thinking about something else. Let's go and have breakfast.'

The next day Anne and Jessica were building a snowman in the back garden when Deirdre O'Connor called out from the door, 'Marianne! Telephone, dearie....'

Anne ran to the house, banging the snow from her boots at the step. She took the kitchen extension. 'Hello?'

'Anne? Jonathan here.'

She was delighted to hear his voice, and her voice was perhaps warmer than she intended. 'How nice to hear from you! How are you?'

'Very well. Any chance of us having dinner together in Charlottetown on Saturday night?'

She thought quickly. David had promised to be back by Saturday afternoon at the latest. 'I think I could manage that,' she said. 'About what time?'

'I'd pick you up around five. We could have dinner at my hotel and then go on to the reception at the art gallery—how would that be?'

'Sounds lovely!'

'It's a black tie affair—have you got an evening dress with you?'

Fortunately she had. 'Perhaps I could change at your hotel,' she suggested, because her dress was definitely not one Miss Winters would wear.

'Sure. Look, my secretary is buzzing me on the other line, Anne, I'll have to go. See you on Saturday.'

'I'm looking forward to it—'bye!'

On Saturday afternoon, watched by an interested Jessica, Anne carefully folded her long dress in tissue paper and put it in her case, adding gold sandals and an evening bag. 'I wish I could see you all dressed up,' Jessica said wistfully.

'Perhaps you can some time, pet. Maybe one evening when your daddy's away we could put on our best dresses and ask Mrs O'Connor to serve our dinner in the dining-room. We could eat by candlelight!'

This idea obviously entranced Jessica. More and more

Anne was aware of how deeply she was growing to love her little daughter; it was a source of infinite joy to her, and she cherished the time they spent together. She gave no thought to the future. The present was happiness enough.

Adding her make-up kit and black evening cloak, she snapped the suitcase shut. 'There, that's done.' She glanced at her watch: four-thirty. She hoped David wouldn't be late, although he surely wouldn't mind if Jessica was left in Mrs O'Connor's care for a short while.

'I trust you're not thinking of leaving us, Miss Winters?'

She looked up, startled. It was as though her thoughts had conjured up David's presence. 'Oh, I'm glad you're back,' she said simply.

For a moment a fleeting expression of what might have been pleasure crossed his face. Then it was gone, so completely that Anne wondered if she had imagined it. Pointedly he eyed her suitcase even as he swung Jessica into his arms. 'I asked you a question.'

Confused, she said, 'Oh—no. But I've been invited out for dinner this evening——'

'With whom?' His voice was a whiplash.

'With a friend of mine from Halifax. He's in Charlotte-town on business,' she answered, trying not to sound defensive.

'And why the suitcase?'

Anne raised her chin defiantly. 'I prefer to change at his hotel.'

There was an edge of contempt in his tone. 'I see,' he said meaningfully.

She blushed scarlet. 'I'm not——'

'From now on I would prefer that you check your arrangements with me beforehand. As it happens, I also have to be out this evening.'

'Mr Metcalfe, you were away when these arrangements were made,' she said crisply, her slim figure tense with anger. 'Furthermore, when I was hired I understood that I would have a certain amount of time off. This will be the first occasion I've left Stornaway since I came——'

'Don't be cross, Anne,' Jessica whimpered.

Anne's eyes flew to the child, who was huddled in David's arms, looking from one adult to the other in bewilderment. Anne was appalled at her own behaviour—to upset Jessica was the last thing in the world she wanted to do. 'I'm sorry, darling,' she said guiltily. 'I did sound cross, didn't I?'

The doorbell chimed, then Deirdre O'Connor's voice floated up the stairs. 'Miss Winter's dearie, your young man's here.'

Jessica's lips quivered. 'Are you coming back? You won't stay away?'

Furious with herself that she had in any way contributed to Jessica's sense of insecurity, Anne was about to speak when David intervened. 'Of course she's coming back, Jess. Tell you what—why don't we go down and meet Marianne's friend, and you can ask him what time they'll be home?' There was a sardonic gleam in his eye as he looked over at Anne, daring her to object.

She wanted nothing more than to poke her tongue out at him. Instead she smiled and said cordially, 'That's a good idea. I'm sure Jonathan would like to meet you both.' She hoped so, because he was not to be given any choice.

The three of them went downstairs together. To the waiting Jonathan they must have looked like a family—the tall, handsome, tawny-haired man with the child in his arms, the slender girl at his side, with her dark hair and serious face.

Anne went ahead of the other two, putting down her case and holding out both hands to the man waiting by the door. All at once he was the one person she needed to see, with his even temper and gentle sense of humour: nice, safe, predictable Jonathan. As different from David as the lamb from the lion.

He bent and kissed her lips with the ease of long familiarity. 'Hi, honey. You look well—the country air must agree with you.'

She smiled back at him. 'You look fine, too,' she said,

for he did look unaccustomedly debonair in his black tuxedo and starched white shirt. 'Jonathan, I'd like you to meet my employer, Mr David Metcalfe, and his daughter Jessica. This is Jonathan Maxwell.'

The two men shook hands and it did not need much discernment to see that they were sizing each other up. 'Good evening, Mr Maxwell,' said David with cool politeness. 'Marianne said you were over here on business?'

'Partly business and partly pleasure.' Jonathan grinned at Anne. 'Later this evening we'll be going to the opening of the new exhibition at Confederation Centre. I'm the director of the Maritime Galleries in Halifax, so I have to attend a certain number of these functions.'

Only Anne had noticed the quick flare of interest in David's eyes at this piece of information, an interest swiftly hidden by his hooded eyelids. 'I see,' he said. 'Apropos that, I think Jessica has a question for you.'

The little girl peered shyly at Jonathan, for once tongue-tied, and finally David came to her rescue. 'She's a bit worried that you might not bring Marianne back,' he said in a level voice.

Jonathan was quick enough to pick up the underlying message, and for a moment open antagonism flared in his normally peaceable eyes. With quiet dignity he said, 'Your daughter need have no worries on that score—I shall take good care of Marianne. I would imagine we'd be back here by midnight at the latest.' He looked at Anne and his eyes softened. 'We'd better get going, hon.'

Anne was equally anxious to be gone. She said to Jessica, 'I'll see you tomorrow, dear.'

Obviously reassured, Jessica held out her arms for a kiss. Anne stepped closer, wishing David would put the child down, but he showed no signs of doing so. She reached up and kissed Jessica's cheek, her body brushing David's his face no distance from hers; she flinched away from the ice-blue of his eyes.

It was a relief to be outdoors. She took a deep breath of the cold night air, and impulsively tucked her arm into

Jonathan's as they walked to the car. He glanced down, pleased by her gesture. 'I've missed you,' he said quietly.

She rubbed her cheek on his shoulder, forgetting that there might be watchers from the house. He put her case in the trunk and then as he opened the car door on her side, kissed her again, with more ardour than usual. She felt no answering passion, but because she was genuinely glad to see him she put her arms around his neck and returned his kiss.

As they drove off, he said with a touch of grimness, 'There's one question I don't need to ask. Jessica's your daughter—she's the image of you.'

'Yes, she is, isn't she? Although she has David's hair colouring.'

'Ah, yes, David—the ex-husband. Did I gather that all was not going smoothly between you? Does he know who you are?'

'I don't think so.'

'You don't sound too sure.'

'Well, he keeps dropping these hints about me resembling someone he used to know—and he was in Fredericton this week, I don't know why.'

'He's a cool customer,' Jonathan said with feeling. 'I wouldn't want to tangle with him.'

'He's a bit overpowering, isn't he?' Anne agreed.

'So what happens now?'

She glanced at him uncertainly. 'What do you mean?'

'Look, I only saw you and Jessica together for five minutes and it didn't take me long to see how strongly you're attached to each other. What are you going to do about it, Anne?'

'Well—nothing at the moment.' Her voice took on colour. 'Jonathan, I'm so enjoying being with her and getting to know her. She's such a delightful child.' She paused thoughtfully. 'To be fair, I guess I have to give David credit for that. Although she badly needs a woman's love. Tonight, for instance, she was frightened that I wasn't going to come back.'

'So are you planning to take up residence with David?' Again that grimness in his tone.

'No, of course not! How could I, even if he does know who I am? I don't love him any more.'

'No?'

'No!' she exploded. 'Our marriage ended four years ago, Jonathan—how many times do I have to tell you that?'

'Okay,' he said heavily. 'Then what about the future, Anne? You love Jessica and Jessica's beginning to love you. Do I have to spell it out? Are you planning to spend the next fifteen years of your life as David's housekeeper?'

'Jonathan, do we have to talk about this now?'

'I think it's high time someone tried to talk a bit of sense to you.' He paused, marshalling his thoughts. 'It seems to me you have three choices: you can tell David who you are and live with him openly as his wife and the mother of his child; you can stay on as a glorified housekeeper and hope people don't notice the likeness between you and Jessica; or you can get out now, before it's too late. Jessica's feelings will no doubt be hurt for a while, but at this stage she'll get over it.'

'And what about me?' Anne whispered.

'You're in as deep as you can be already, aren't you?' He banged his gloved hand against the steering wheel. 'Oh, Anne, I hate to say "I told you so", but I did warn you how badly you could be hurt in this situation.' He looked over at her with a worried frown on his brow, and she sensed his anger was more on her behalf than directed at her. 'I don't want to see you hurt. Of course, there's one other choice—is there any chance David would give you custody of the child?'

'No, I'm sure there isn't,' she said with absolute conviction. 'Besides, Jessica's lived with him all her life. It would be cruel to take her away from him.'

'It's a mess, isn't it, hon? And I don't see any easy solution. I still think the best thing would be for you to leave right away—at least you know now your child didn't die four years ago, and that she's being well looked after.'

'I can't, Jonathan!' It was a cry from the heart. 'You may well be right—it might be the best thing for all of us. But I just can't....' She rubbed her eyes. 'Oh damn, I'm crying!'

Jonathan pulled over to the side of the road and waited for her to collect herself. Finally she gave him a watery grin. 'Sorry.'

He patted her hand. 'It's all right. Let's drop it for now. But if you do decide to leave, I'll be there to look after you, Anne, you know that, don't you?'

'Yes—thank you, Jonathan.'

He drove on, purposely changing the subject to that of a young artist he had met on the west coast. Gradually they drifted back into the easy companionship they had always shared; the tensions of the past hour were put aside. They had a pleasant and relaxing dinner together at Jonathan's hotel and then went up to his room so Anne could change for the reception.

She shut herself in the bathroom and began getting ready. Although her role as the subdued Miss Winters had not seriously bothered her vanity, it was still fun to be able to dress as she pleased. She started by sweeping her hair high on her head, leaving a few stray tendrils to curl about her ears and neck ... dark green eyeshadow, mascara to lengthen the thick fringe of her lashes, a warm apricot lipstick on the curve of her mouth ... the jade earrings and a matching necklace that Jonathan had given her. Her dress was fashioned of jade green silk; it was high-waisted with full sleeves and a low-cut square neckline. Its severity of style subtly emphasised the feminine curves of her figure while her skin looked creamy-white against the rich shadings of the fabric.

As she came back into the bedroom, Jonathan looked up. He sat quite still, staring at her. 'You look magnificent,' he said huskily, then a strange expression of pain crossed his face. 'You're too beautiful for me, Anne—you belong with someone like David Metcalfe. Not with someone ordinary like me.'

It was a totally unexpected thing for him to say; it was not like Jonathan to belittle himself. She wondered how she would be feeling if it were David waiting for her, but it was a feat beyond her imagination. 'Don't say that, Jonathan, I dressed like this for you, not for David.'

To her relief he smiled at her, his old self again. 'In that case, let's go and knock their eyes out!'

When they arrived, the gallery was already crowded with the invited guests; there was the clink of glasses and a well-bred hum of voices. After Jonathan had procured them both drinks, he and Anne immediately became part of a group of his friends. During the next hour Anne met a confusing array of people and although she enjoyed talking to them, she was increasingly anxious to wander around the gallery looking at the paintings. Then she noticed that Jonathan had become engrossed in a business conversation with two other men; he would not miss her. She murmured her excuses to the others and with a delightful feeling of truancy headed for the far wall. She would start there and work her way round.

The third painting she looked at captured her complete attention; not very large, done in oils, it depicted three children in brightly coloured snowsuits skating on the frozen surface of a lake. Against the cold grey winter background, the vivid hues of the children's clothing glowed like jewels.

'It's beautiful, isn't it?'

She was so absorbed that for a moment all she did was to nod her agreement. Then she recognised the deep timbre of the voice. With a strange feeling of fatality, she turned around; it was with no surprise that she saw David standing there. In silence they regarded each other.

He was in tailored evening clothes that fitted him to perfection. Although this was highly civilised garb, he moved with an animal grace, like some sleek jungle cat, dangerous and powerful. He was, she decided faintly, easily the most handsome man she had ever seen; she would have to be dead in her grave not to feel the pull of his intense virility.

As for him, he saw a slim, creamy-skinned creature with eyes of emerald-green and a crown of lustrous dark hair. The medieval simplicity of her dress gave her a seductive and wholly feminine allure.

For once there was no mockery in his tone. 'You knew I would be here.'

'Yes.' And at some deep subconscious level she had known it, ever since he had betrayed that flash of interest in her whereabouts tonight. So perhaps what she had told Jonathan had not been strictly true: perhaps she had not dressed just for him.

'I was invited two weeks ago. But I hadn't planned to attend until I knew you'd be here.'

Her heart began to beat with suffocatingly heavy strokes. What did he mean by that? Why had he come? Silently he held out his arm and equally silently she took it, her ringless fingers white against his sleeve. Together they began to look at the paintings.

Gradually, as they progressed around the room, Anne relaxed, for although she was no nearer to understanding the mystery of his presence, it no longer seemed to matter. She gave herself up to enjoying David's company: the accuracy of his judgments, the breadth of his knowledge, the occasional rapier flash of his wit. With increasing confidence she began to make her own responses, delighted when more than once she made him laugh.

It was with a sense of shock that she saw Jonathan approach them; she had forgotten all about him. 'Good evening, Mr Metcalfe. Anne, a group of us are going to the cocktail lounge at the hotel. Are you ready to go now?'

She did not even notice that he had called her 'Anne'. She knew she didn't want to go, but equally well knew she had no choice. 'Yes—of course,' she stammered.

'Will you join us, Mr Metcalfe?' Although Jonathan was being punctiliously polite, there was no real warmth in his invitation.

'Thank you, no—I'd better head back to Stornaway.

Perhaps you'd prefer to come back with me now, Marianne?
It would save Mr Maxwell the drive.'

Her sharp longing to do as he asked horrified her. 'No,
Jonathan will bring me home,' she said firmly, quite unaware of the hint of wistfulness in her expressive face.

'I'll bid you both goodnight, then,' David said with a
sardonic little bow. Anne found herself watching him as he
strode across the room; more than one woman's head
turned to follow his progress.

She gave herself a mental shake and turned to Jonathan,
saying with a brightness that did not deceive him at all,
'Shall we go?'

The cocktail bar was crowded and noisy, the air smoke-
laden. The throb of music and the flash of coloured lights
came from a disco group on the small stage. Anne looked
around her in faint desperation; she felt disorientated and
at odds with herself. She did not understand the sense of
closeness that had flowered between her and David in the
gallery; remembering it was painful, for it had been like the
perfect companionship of the early days of their marriage
... what she did understand, and felt helpless to amend,
was that she was hurting Jonathan. He was in love with
her and wanted to marry her, and he must surely see how
she was drifting further and further away from him, caught
up in the loving relationship with her daughter ... and
now he had seen evidence that she was not immune to the
powerful pull of David's personality. What had Jonathan's
first piece of advice been? 'Tell David who you are and live
with him openly as his wife and the mother of his daughter ...' Oh God, how could that ever happen? And yet, for
Jessica's sake, how perfect a solution it would be....

Someone thrust a drink in her hand and she made an
effort to come back to the present. She drank it down too
quickly and started on a second; she danced with a succes-
sion of different men, none of whom she could have put a
name to five minutes later, talking to them all with a kind
of feverish gaiety; somehow she found herself on her third
drink. Jonathan seemed to have deserted her. The evening

became a nightmare of noise and flashing lights and strangers' faces. She wanted to go home, she thought forlornly. It seemed natural to think of Stornaway as home ... recklessly she emptied her glass again.

Someone took it from her hand—Jonathan. 'You've had enough,' he said abruptly. 'Sorry I left you on your own, but I've just made a really important contract for my business. We'd better leave—it's nearly one-thirty.'

She got up, leaning heavily on his arm. Afterwards she had no recollection of leaving the bar, or of getting to his car, or even of the drive home. It was the cessation of motion that made her open her eyes. 'Where are we?' she said muzzily.

'Stornaway.'

'Already?' She blinked at him. He looked tired and there were unusual lines of strain around his mouth. She made an effort to pull herself together. 'Jonathan, I'm sorry——'

'Hush,' he said firmly. 'Don't apologise. Do what you have to do, Anne, and if you need me at any time of the day or night, just pick up the telephone.'

'You're too good for me,' she mumbled.

'Nonsense. Do you want me to come in with you, or can you manage?'

'I'll be all right.' She leaned over to kiss him, feeling her head swirl as she did so. Then she was out of the car and watching the red gleam of his tail-lights disappear down the driveway.

CHAPTER FIVE

THE night air struck her like a blow, while the stars in the velvet sky dipped and swayed. Very carefully she walked towards the front door, her suitcase banging awkwardly against her leg. She felt as though she were floating; it was a relief to grab hold of the door handle. But as she did so the door swung open and she would have fallen but for the strong grasp of the man standing there. It was, of course, David. He took the suitcase from her unresisting fingers, put in on the floor and closed the door behind her.

Anne focussed on him with some difficulty. He had discarded his jacket but was still wearing the narrow-fitting dark trousers and the crisp white shirt he had had on earlier; the shirt was unbuttoned at the neck, with the sleeves rolled up to the elbows. He was, she realised with a sinking sensation in the pit of her stomach, in a towering rage.

She closed her eyes, wishing he would go away. Whatever she had been drinking at the cocktail lounge had been different from what she had drunk at the reception, and earlier she had had wine with her dinner—no wonder she felt so awful.

'You're drunk,' David said coldly.

Her eyes snapped open. 'I am not!'

'Do you have to get drunk in order to go to bed with someone?'

She leaned back against the oak-panelled door; it felt comfortingly solid. 'I am not drunk and I have not been to bed with anyone,' she said, enunciating as clearly as she could.

'You were leaving the reception at ten-thirty to go to your friend's hotel. It's now two-thirty. So what the hell did you do in the meantime?'

'Get drunk,' she said pertly.

His mouth tightened. 'For someone who promised Jessica you'd be home at midnight, you're not doing very well, are you?'

She was terrified by the savagery in his tone. A wave of nausea engulfed her and grimly she fought it back. That would be the final humiliation....

'Come here,' he ordered.

Spellbound by his penetrating blue eyes, Anne pushed herself upright and walked towards him, holding herself steady with a kind of desperate pride. He stared down at her. Her cloak was slipping from her shoulder and her skin gleamed palely against its black folds. Her eyes shone a luminous grey-green in a paper-white face. She was swaying on her feet. With a sensuality that made her senses swim David ran his finger down the length of her neck, then across the swell of her bosom to lie in the hollow between her breasts. 'When I take you to bed, my dear,' he said with lazy deliberation, 'you will be stone cold sober. And you will be willing—oh yes, you'll be willing.'

Panic-stricken, she tried to move away from him, but her limbs would not obey her. Then his mouth was upon hers, brutal, probing, forcing a response from her. She beat ineffectually at his chest with her fists, trying to wrench her head away, but his hands were tangled in her hair and she was caught as helpless in his steel grip as an animal in a trap.

Darkness enveloped her, a darkness shot with light. The lights whirled and spun, faster and faster, carrying her with them ... with a tiny moan she collapsed in his arms.

Against her cheek she felt the warmth of someone else's body, although the rest of her was bitterly cold. She opened her eyes, fighting her way back to reality through a dense black fog. She was being carried—and it was David who was carrying her. She made a convulsive movement of protest, and heard his voice say quietly, 'You fainted. Just be still.'

It seemed the natural thing to obey him. Her cheek, she

now realised, was lying against his shirtfront; she could feel the slow, steady beat of his heart, infinitely comforting. He pushed open a door and then she felt herself being lowered on to a bed. She tried to sit up, but dizziness swept over her again so that she fell back on the pillow. For some reason it seemed important to her that she be honest with him. 'You were quite right,' she whispered. 'I did have too much to drink. I didn't want to go back to the hotel lounge, I just wanted to come home.'

'With me.'

'Yes.'

She felt him undo the delicate straps of her gold sandals, and slide them off her feet. 'Sit up,' he ordered.

'I can't.'

He gave a smothered sound that might have been laughter, then his arm was around her shoulders, holding her in a sitting position. Her head fell forward on his shoulder, fitting in the curve of his collarbone. His skin smelled clean and sweet, indefinably masculine. He unhooked her cloak, then she heard the metallic sound of a zipper. She stiffened, pushing herself away from him. 'Don't,' she protested weakly.

'My dear girl, I'm not going to leave you lying on the bed in your evening dress. Apart from anything else, what do you think Jessica would make of that when she comes to wake you up tomorrow—or rather today?'

Anne groaned audibly.

'And you're going to have one hell of a hangover,' he added.

'Don't sound so pleased about it,' she muttered. He had pulled the zipper all the way down. She could feel his hands on her back and arms, taking off her dress; they felt like fingers of fire and she shivered with pleasure.

'You'll have to stand up,' he said emotionlessly. Without thinking of the consequences she did so. The dress fell in heavy folds to the floor, leaving her clad only in a wisp of strapless bra and lacy panties; she saw how his eyes lingered over the fullness of her breasts, the curve of her waist and hips, before dragging themselves back to her face. Yet his hands on her shoulders, pushing her back on the bed, were as impersonal as a brother's.

He hung up the dress in her closet. 'Where's your night-dress?'

'Under my pillow. I—I can manage now.'

'I'm not leaving here until I see you in bed.'

'Turn your back, then,' she said crossly. He did so, and she awkwardly stripped off her flimsy underclothes and pulled her nightdress over her head. It was made of pale green nylon and in its way was almost as revealing as her underclothes.

David turned around again, and as though he had been doing it for years began pulling the pins from her hair, so that it fell in soft waves around her face. 'There, you'll do. Into bed with you!'

As though I was five years old, Anne thought crossly. But then she remembered his eyes on her body, and felt a trembling begin within her. She slid her legs under the covers and lay back, her hair a dark cloud on the pillow. 'David——' she whispered.

He had been bending over her to pull up the blankets. The light from the hall fell obliquely on his face, casting shadows under his deepset eyes. throwing into relief the chiselled line of his mouth. All her normal caution deserted her. She slid her arms around his neck and pulled his head down. His weight fell across her as she began kissing him, slowly, sensuously, exposing all her pent-up need of him.

Later, she had no idea for how long he yielded to her: it could have been only seconds or it could have been minutes. However brief a time it was, while it lasted they were in one accord in their mutual desire. Then, with the shock of an ice-cold wave, she felt him pull free of her embrace. As he knelt over her, she could hear the harshness of his breathing.

'Oh, no, Marianne,' he grated. 'I'm not getting into your bed that way. What's the matter—didn't your friend Jona-than satisfy you?'

Pain ripped through her, driving the air from her lungs so that she was temporarily speechless. She cowered back on the mattress, her hands falling limply to her sides.

'Don't ever try to seduce me again—I'm too experienced to fall into that trap.'

'But you wanted me. For a minute you wanted me—you can't deny that.'

'I'm only human,' he drawled. Indolently he ran his eyes up and down her body. 'But I draw the line at second-hand goods.'

'Get out!' she cried, incoherent with mingled rage and pain. 'Get out of my room—and don't come back!'

Lithely David got to his feet. Because his face was in darkness, she could not see his expression, but his voice chilled her to the bone. 'I'll see you in my study before lunch and we'll finish this discussion then. Should Jessica ask, you returned before midnight.' He went out, closing the door behind him and leaving her alone in the darkness, with tears trickling down her cheeks.

It seemed only minutes before Anne was rudely awakened by Jessica, who burst in her door and bounced up on the bed. 'Wake up! It's morning—you're a sleepyhead!'

Anne groaned and rolled over on her stomach, burying her face in the pillow. 'What time is it?' she grumbled. 'Oh, Jess, don't bounce so hard—I've got a headache.'

'Dee-dee's bringing your breakfast. That'll make it better,' the child said confidently.

Anne was not so sure, the thought of food being far from appealing. She rolled over again, giving Jessica a weak smile. 'You're all dressed,' she managed to say admiringly, for this was one of Jessica's more recent accomplishments.

Deirdre poked her head around the door, saw that Anne was awake and put the tray by the bed. 'There you are, dearie. Mr Metcalfe asked me to remind you that he'll be in the study all morning.'

And that was really enough to spoil her appetite, thought Anne with a kind of desperate humour, looking at the contents of the tray without much enthusiasm.

'Can I have a piece of your orange?' Jessica asked hopefully.

'By all means—help yourself.' She took a sip of black coffee, and began to eat the thinly sliced toast.

'Aren't you having any jam?'

'Not this morning. Why don't you have it on that other piece of toast?'

Between them they managed to empty the tray, so that at least Deirdre would not be asking questions about Anne's lack of appetite. Then Anne shooed Jessica out of the room, and had a steaming hot shower. She dressed in a rose pink tweed skirt and a matching sweater, not feeling in the mood for the more sedate grey and beige outfits hanging in her cupboard. After last night it didn't seem to matter much what she wore anyway.... As she brushed her hair dry, she found herself staring at her reflection in the mirror. She had, unfortunately, a very clear recollection of the events of last night, particularly of her attempt to get David into bed with her—how could she have done it? Shame suffused her cheeks with colour; it was bad enough that she had tried to seduce him, but even harder to accept was the fact that he had rejected her. Oh, damn, damn, damn, why had she done it? That would teach her to mix her drinks.... She looked at herself with acute disfavour, seeing smudges of weariness under her eyes, her face an unhealthy white. She looked awful. And in a few minutes she would have to go downstairs and face David.

For the first time she wondered what he wanted. There were a number of possibilities, none of them pleasant. Perhaps he had tried to check on Marianne Winters' references in Fredericton, in which case she was in trouble, with no way to extricate herself that she could think of. Perhaps David was afraid Jessica was getting too dependent on her— her eyes darkened with panic. Perhaps after her admittedly atrocious behaviour last night, he was going to dismiss her, for he would hardly consider as a fit companion for his daughter someone who drank too much and then tried to seduce her employer. What on earth would she do if he fired her? The mere contemplation of this opened in front of her an abyss of horror. She couldn't bear to leave Jessica—she would do almost anything to prevent that happening.

By now she was in a pitiable state of anxiety, her palms damp, her throat tight with tension. Twice she smudged her lipstick, and then she dropped her favourite compact on the bathroom floor, where it shattered into pieces. Oh dear, she thought hopelessly, she shouldn't have got up this morning at all.

Finally she could delay no longer. Head held high, she walked downstairs and tapped on the study door. A deep voice bade her enter. David was seated at the desk, a welter of paperwork spread out on its surface. 'Close the door, would you mind?' he said casually. 'Then sit down. I'll be right with you, I just want to finish this up first.' He bent his head over his correspondence again.

She perched on the hearth, her hands spread to the bright crackle of flames, somewhat encouraged by his off-hand tone of voice; he did not sound like someone who was about to dismiss an employee. Unless, of course, her presence or absence at Stornaway was a matter of indifference to him ... unconsciously a worried frown creased her forehead as she gazed into the fire.

'Can I pour you a sherry?'

She shuddered visibly. 'No, thank you!'

'You look remarkably well, all things considered.'

She glowered at him. He was leaning against the mantel, completely relaxed, his blue eyes derisive. He looked disturbingly handsome in a cream silk shirt and close-fitting beige trousers fashioned of supple suede. 'If you're going to tell me off, do it and get it over with,' she said truculently.

'I did not necessarily bring you here to tell you off. After all, why should I? You only proved my point, that there's more to the correct Miss Winters than meets the eye.'

For two cents she would have given him her opinion of the dreary Miss Winters, but forcibly she curbed her tongue, since she was in enough trouble as it was.

'Which reminds me—you didn't seem to be having any trouble seeing those paintings last night without your glasses.'

Sweetly she fluttered her eyelashes at him. 'Have you never heard of contact lenses, Mr Metcalfe?'

'Come now, Marianne, surely after last night you can bring yourself to call me David?'

Hot colour flooded her face. Unable to meet his eyes, she looked down at her lap.

'I would, by the way, prefer not to have a repetition of any of the events of last night,' he went on smoothly. 'In a week or two I'll make arrangements for you to have three or four days off. It would probably be best if you spent them away from here, in Halifax, for instance. I don't think Jessica should come to depend on you totally.'

She sat quietly, although anger burned within her. What gave him the right to arrange her life for her? In a colourless voice she said, 'Very well. Is there anything else?'

'I don't believe——' The telephone rang on his desk, startling Anne. 'Excuse me for a minute.' He picked up the receiver, and although she tried not to listen it was impossible not to hear his side of the conversation. 'Hello?' His voice warmed. 'Oh, Sonja. I've been wondering when I'd hear from you ever since I got your letter.... You're there now, are you? You must have come in on the Montreal flight? ... Okay, I can be there in forty-five minutes ... you can stay a few days, I hope? ... Good, I'll look forward to seeing you. 'Bye, darling.'

He turned to face Anne. 'That was a friend of mine,' he explained, somewhat unnecessarily Anne felt. 'Sonja Sorensen. She'd written to say she'd be comiing for a few days, but she wasn't sure of the exact date. She's at the airport now, so I'll go and get her. Would you mind asking Mrs O'Connor to prepare the guest room, please? It's the room across the hall from mine.'

'All right,' she said, rather ungraciously. 'Was that all you wanted to discuss with me?'

David shrugged into a suede jacket, checking for his car keys, his mind obviously not on Anne. 'I think that was all,' he said vaguely. 'You won't forget to speak to Deirdre?'

'I've said I'll do it.' Resentfully she felt as though she had been relegated to the role of servant, but there was nothing she could do about it. Not bothering to say good-bye, he left the room, and in a moment she heard the Mercedes pull out of the garage.

Anne's main feeling was one of anti-climax; she had been so frightened before this disconcertingly brief interview, prepared for the worst. She shouldn't have been such a pessimist. He obviously hadn't checked on her references in Fredericton, and it didn't seem as though he had any intention of firing her. All he wanted her to do was spend three or four days in Halifax. She'd never understand the man . . . be that as it may, it would seem that she was safe, and that was a relief. She got up from her seat by the fire and went in search of Mrs O'Connor, whom she eventually located in the pantry, making a sandwich for Jessica.

'Mr Metcalfe asked that the guest room across from his room'—why did that rankle?—'be prepared, Deirdre.'

'Now who would be coming to visit?' the older woman asked, openly inquisitive.

'A Miss Sonja Sorensen.'

'Is she? Well now, that's very interesting! Yes, I can check on the room in a minute and put out fresh towels. Did he say how long she'd be staying?'

'No, he didn't.' Unwillingly Anne's curiosity got the better of her. 'Has she been here before?'

'Oh, yes, indeed.'

'I don't like her,' Jessica said flatly.

'Jessica!' Anne exclaimed, faintly horrified. 'You shouldn't say things like that.'

'Why not? It's true,' Jessica replied, with the irrefutable logic of the very young.

Feeling that she shouldn't leave the matter there, but not really knowing what else to say, Anne added; 'Your father went to get her at the airport. Make sure that you're polite to her, even if you don't like her.'

'I hope Daddy won't be long. He promised to take me skiing after lunch.'

'He didn't say when he'd be back.'

'He'd better not be late,' said Jessica, the eyes that were so like Anne's a mutinous grey.

But he was late. Lunch time came and went and there was no sign of him. Jessica, normally such a good-natured child, became more and more fractious as the afternoon progressed. Nothing would satisfy her. Anne knew the child's bad temper was only an expression of disappointment, but even so it was difficult to deal with. Anne did get her outdoors with the toboggan, but first Jessica's hands were cold, then there was snow in her boots, and finally, 'I don't want to toboggan with you, I want to ski with Daddy!'

Anne said, 'Okay, that's enough, Jessica. I don't want to hear the word "skiing" again!' The child looked at her in dismay, for Anne had never been so harsh with her before. 'We'll go indoors now,' Anne went on, not giving Jessica the chance to object. 'We'll light the fire in your room, and we'll make toast and cocoa on the fire, and colour in your new colouring book. Come along.' And she took Jessica by the hand.

This unaccustomed firmness worked wonders. Although subdued at first, Jessica soon entered into the spirit of things, and presently she was sitting on the sheepskin rug by the fireplace, licking crumbs from her fingers, a brown rim of cocoa around her mouth. They had blackened the bottom of a saucepan, burned three pieces of toast and Anne's finger, but seeing the sparkle back in Jessica's eyes, Anne knew it had been worth it. Gleefully Jessica tipped open her box of crayons, so that they spilled all over the rug. She began sorting them into two piles. 'One for you and one for me ...'

'Oh, there you are,' came David's voice from the door. 'We were looking for you.'

For once Jessica did not run to meet him. 'You didn't take me skiing,' she accused.

David looked disconcerted. With swift discernment

Anne knew he had completely forgotten about the skiing
expedition; the phone call from Sonja had driven it out of
his mind. She felt a flare of anger—or at least she called it
anger.

'I'm sorry, sweetheart,' David said, 'I forgot all about it.
Tell you what—we'll go first thing tomorrow morning,
how would that be?'

'Okay—you won't forget again?'

'No, I promise.' Father and daughter smiled at each
other, amity restored between them, and Anne felt the
familiar catch in her throat. Then David added, 'Say hello
to Sonja, Jess.'

With a gravity that made Anne want to laugh, Jessica repeated obediently, 'Hello, Sonja.'

'And this is Miss Marianne Winters, Sonja, who looks
after Jessica for me. Marianne—Miss Sonja Sorensen.'

'How do you do, Miss Sorensen?' said Anne, favouring
the other woman with her wide, friendly smile.

But Sonja only nodded, her eyes already sliding dismis-
sively away from Anne to survey the litter of dishes and
crayons on the carpet. 'You don't get any tidier, Jessica,'
she remarked in her charmingly accented voice. 'What have
you been doing?'

'We made cocoa,' Jessica said sulkily. 'And Anne burned
her finger.'

'Did you?' David said sharply to Anne. 'Let me see.'

'Really, it's nothing,' she disclaimed.

He strode over to the rug, kneeling beside her. 'Show
me, I said.' She held out her hand with the angry red burn
on her middle finger. 'There's some ointment in the first-
aid kit in the bathroom—make sure you put some on,' he
ordered.

'To make cocoa like that seems rather a dangerous and
silly thing to do anyway,' Sonja interjected. 'Couldn't you
have made it in the kitchen?'

'She's quite right—it was a crazy thing to do. You could
have burned yourself a lot worse than that,' said David, an
edge of anger in his voice.

Anne was determined not to start a squabble in front of Jessica, and equally determined that he would hear about this later. 'I'm sorry,' she said with an assumed humility that made his eyes narrow suspiciously. 'It won't happen again.'

As David admired Jessica's picture, Anne found herself studying the woman by the door, for already Anne was agreeing with Jessica—she did not like Sonja Sorensen. She was incredibly beautiful, though—tall and statuesque with a breathtaking figure and the true Nordic colouring: a sheaf of pale blonde hair coiled on her head, cool blue eyes, perfect features. She was wearing a cream-coloured mink coat with matching leather boots, over an ice-blue cashmere skirt and sweater; she was as chic—and as bored-looking— as a *Vogue* model. It was impossible for Anne not to glance down at her own attire: faded blue jeans, and a pink mohair sweater that had seen better days. Her hair was in a pony-tail, her glasses were on her nose, and her face innocent of make-up, and probably still showing the ravages of last night. No wonder the elegant Miss Sorensen had hardly noticed her! Not that Sonja Sorensen would ever pay much attention to a paid companion—such people would be beneath her notice.

The tall blonde shifted restlessly. 'David, are you going to be much longer?'

David had been chatting away to Jessica, perhaps to make amends for his forgetfulness, Anne thought. He looked up. 'Sorry, Sonja, I'm neglecting you, aren't I? I'll only be a minute. Maybe Marianne wouldn't mind showing you to your room. Then at least you can hang your coat up and look as though you've come to stay for a while.'

Sonja gave him an intimate little smile, that disappeared instantly as David turned back to Jessica. Seething inwardly for reasons she did not analyse, Anne led the way down the hall. There was a door directly across from David's room. How very convenient, Anne thought cynically. Pushing it open, she ushered Sonja in. A set of matching luggage, also cream-coloured, was neatly piled by the canopied double bed. It was a far more feminine room than her own, with ruffled bedspread and drapes, a flowered rug, and delicate French provincial furniture. There seemed to be an over-abundance of fussy ornaments and floral prints—a room at odds with the rest of the house, Anne decided, rather puzzled.

Sonja solved the mystery. 'I decorated this room myself,' she announced. 'When David bought the house, he allowed me to choose the furnishings for my room. It is delightful, is it not?'

'Yes, it is,' Anne agreed politely, if not very truthfully.

'I'm glad you are working here,' said Sonja, sitting down at the dresser and taking out her compact. 'With you to look after Jessica, David and I will have more time alone to-gether. The last time I was here, the child trailed every-where with us.'

It would appear that Sonja had no more liking for Jessica than Jessica for Sonja; Anne might have been amused but for the complete indifference with which Sonja spoke—Jessica's feelings were plainly of no importance to Sonja. 'Don't you like Jessica?' Anne asked, keeping her voice carefully neutral.

Sonja shrugged, applying a touch of lipstick to her already perfectly outlined lips. 'I don't like or dislike her—she's a child, and children are generally a nuisance. Always underfoot, always wanting attention. And David is be-sotted with her. It's not healthy for a man to be so wrapped up in his daughter.'

To her amazement, Anne found herself springing to David's defence. 'He's not besotted with her,' she said, not quite succeeding in hiding her irritation. 'But he does love her. I think he's a good father—he has a lot of fun with her, but he can be strict as well.'

Sonja looked shrewdly at the other girl. 'How fiercely you defend him,' she said in an amused voice, although her eyes remained cold and watchful. 'Don't be so foolish as to fall in love with him, will you, Miss Winters? He's a very handsome man, and leaves a trail of broken hearts wherever he goes. But always he comes back to me—don't forget that.'

'The sheer effrontery of the woman made Anne gasp. 'I have no intention of falling in love with him,' she said roundly. 'In fact, there are a number of things about him I thoroughly dislike. But now it's my turn to pass out some advice—don't come between David and his daughter, Miss Sorensen. Apart from the hurt it could cause Jessica, it would be a stupid and shortsighted thing to do. David loves his daughter and will appreciate you the less if you try to disrupt that relationship.'

'You're impertinent, Miss Winters!'

Unrepentantly Anne said, 'You started this conversation, not I.'

'I shall speak to David about your rudeness.'

'What's all this about?' David himself was standing in the doorway.

'Ah, David.' Somehow Sonja contrived to look pathetic. 'Miss Winters presumes to tell me how I should behave with Jessica. You know I care for your daughter—I spoke about cooking the food over the fire only because I didn't want to see Jessica hurt.'

Anne was appalled by how cleverly Sonja had twisted the truth. 'We were not——'

'Really, Marianne, I will not tolerate rudeness to my guests, whether you think there's provocation or not,' David said curtly. 'You must learn to take criticism. The fact that you burned yourself shows the danger of what you were doing.'

Her voice trembling with suppressed anger, Anne said, 'I'm tired of hearing about the so-called dangers of toasting a bit of bread over the fire. The reason I suggested it to Jessica in the first place was because she was so disappointed about *your* failure to keep your promise to take her skiing. She was being extremely difficult to handle and I was having a hard time with her——'

'That's what I pay you for,' David interrupted, his blue eyes blazing with an anger that matched her own.

'However much you're paying her, I think it's too much,' Sonja said acidly. 'She acts above her station. She's only an au pair girl, after all. I'd get rid of her if I were you.',

How Anne longed to tell the truth—that she was Jessica's mother, and in the eyes of the law still very much David's wife. That would put Miss Sonja Sorensen's beautiful nose out of joint, she thought pettishly. But it was impossible to do so. In frustrated silence she glared at the other woman, her only source of satisfaction that at least David couldn't marry Sonja—not until he divorced her, Anne. How Jessica would hate having Sonja for a stepmother!

As her temper subsided, she began to realise that, unwisely, she had made an enemy in Sonja. She had no idea how much influence Sonja had over David; she would just have to hope that her own position would not be jeopardised by Sonja's antagonism. She suddenly knew that she had had enough of all this. 'If I said anything to upset you, Miss Sorensen,' she said with quiet dignity, 'then I apologise. I didn't intend to be rude. Now, if you'll both excuse me, I'll go back to my job of looking after Jessica.'

Her head held high, she walked towards the door. Stormy grey eyes met piercing blue ones, and it was hers that fell. She brushed past David, her truant memory choosing that moment to remind her that only last night she had tried to seduce the man. She must have been crazy, she thought bitterly. To David she was nothing but an employee, and a recalcitrant one at that. She'd do well to keep that in mind.

CHAPTER SIX

ONLY Jessica and David went on the skiing expedition the next morning. David had not invited Anne to go, making it clear that it was strictly a father–daughter outing; and Sonja was not yet out of bed. If there were implications to be drawn from that, Anne chose to ignore them. She spent a quiet morning in the study, reading and writing a couple of letters, and trying not to mind the loneliness of being left out of David's and Jessica's plans. It was one of those mornings when the anomalies of her position struck home: she loved Jessica with a mother's love, but outwardly she could behave only as the paid companion. As Marianne Winters she should be delighted to have a morning off duty—as Anne Metcalfe, she wanted to be with her daughter.

However, in the afternoon David and Sonja disappeared somewhere, so Anne had Jessica to herself. The child slept for an hour after lunch, then woke up full of energy. 'Let's go for a walk down by the river,' Anne suggested. 'Didn't you tell me there were often ducks down there?'

Jessica was agreeable, so after dressing in snowsuits and boots, the two of them set off. It was one of those deceptive days in the middle of winter when the Canadian climate played tricks: had Anne not known it was January, she could have sworn it was April. The temperature was well above freezing and the row of icicles along the garage roof dripped with a monotonous regularity. The snow was becoming wet and heavy, perfect for snowballs, and their mittens were soon snow-caked.

They slithered down the hill towards the river. The open channel was wider today, reflecting the blue of the sky. A pair of mergansers were drifting with the current, occasionally diving for food. Further downstream Anne could see a flock of golden-eyes. It was a peaceful scene, punctuated only by the trickle of melting ice and the swish of snow sliding from the boughs of spruce trees in the nearby woods. While Jessica amused herself trying to dam up a little rivulet that was running down the hill, Anne stood quietly, enjoying the peace and quiet.

It was then that she heard the sound—a faint whimper of pain. She glanced swiftly at Jessica, wondering if it was one of her tricks, but the child was absorbed in her dam-building project. She strained her ears. There it was again. It was coming from the woods. 'Did you hear that, Jess?'

'What?'

'Listen a minute.' Again the cry from the woods, although it seemed weaker this time. 'Come on,' Anne said decisively, 'we'd better go and see what it is.'

Hand in hand they approached the thicket, which was a tangle of alders and young spruce growing close to the riverbank. Ducking under the branches, hampered by the deep snow, they were guided by a volley of whimpers and cries—whatever it was had obviously sensed their presence. 'It sounds like a dog,' Anne said breathlessly, holding up a sharp-pointed branch so Jessica could go underneath.

She was right: it was a dog. A big black dog, gaunt and unkempt, who wagged his tail frantically as he saw them coming. 'Stay back, Jess, until I see what's the matter,' Anne ordered. She approached cautiously, for although the dog looked friendly enough, one could never be sure. 'Oh dear,' she said in distress, 'it's foot is caught in a trap. Poor thing!'

Forgetting her caution. she knelt in the snow. A sharp-toothed steel trap about six inches across had clamped shut over the dog's front leg, and she winced at the sight of the ugly wound, caked with dried blood. Taking off her mittens, she tried to force the jaws of the trap apart, but she couldn't move it even a fraction of an inch. Red-faced from her exertions, she gave a sigh of exasperation. 'What'll we do, Jessica? I can't budge it.'

She sat back on her heels, absently patting the dog's shoulder; his bones were sharp under the slack skin.

'Daddy could fix it,' Jessica said confidently.

'Jessica, you're a marvel!' As though the dog could understand her, Anne said clearly, 'We'll be back in half an hour—okay?'

The dog howled piteously as they struggled back through the trees. 'He thinks we're not coming back,' said Jessica, her lip trembling.

'But we are. So let's hurry, because the quicker we can get home, the quicker we'll be back.' As they clambered up the hillside, Anne was surprised to see the sun sinking to the horizon—they'd been gone for quite a while. She hoped David was home. If he wasn't, she didn't know what she'd do.

They went in the back door and quickly Anne pulled off Jessica's boots and soaking wet snowsuit, removing her own boots as well. Then they hurried through the kitchen and out into the hall. From the study came the murmur of voices. The door was open.

Anne walked in, her eyes flying to the tall figure in his favourite position by the mantel. 'Oh, David!' she exclaimed warmly, 'I'm so glad you're home!'

There was a spark of indefinable emotion in his deepset eyes. 'Oh, why?'

Unceremoniously Jessica pushed past Anne. 'Daddy, you've got to come! There's a dog and his foot's caught in a trap and he can't get it out——'

As Anne followed Jessica further into the room, she felt her heart sink. David and Sonja were obviously going out, for he was wearing an impeccably tailored dark grey business suit and Sonja an elegant turquoise cocktail dress, with diamonds flashing at her ears and on her wrist.

Sonja raised her eyebrows at the child's intrusion and before David could speak said coldly, 'Miss Winters, it's time you taught the child some manners. That is, if you're capable of it.'

There was a deadly little silence, while Anne held tightly to her fraying temper. 'Jessica's upset,' she said. 'There's a dog caught in a trap down by the river. I wasn't strong enough to spring the trap, so we came up here to get some help.'

'Well, it will have to wait until morning,' Sonja said indifferently. 'We're about to go out for dinner, aren't we, darling?'

Jessica's face fell and without warning she burst into tears, turning around and flinging herself at Anne. 'Hush, pet,' Anne said soothingly. Looking over at David and making no attempt to keep the disillusion from her face, she went on, 'Please will you give me the phone number of someone who *would* be willing to go back with me? I can't leave the dog there all night—it's suffering, and half starved.'

'You're both jumping to conclusions. I don't recall saying that I wouldn't go.'

'You mean you will?' Anne said hopefully.

'Of course I will,' he said in irritation. 'I'm not completely heartless. Jessica, stop crying. I'll go and change, then Anne and I will go down and bring the dog back. You'll have to wait here while we're gone, it's getting too dark for you to be out again.'

Jessica raised a tear-streaked face, an incongruously radiant smile already dawning on it. 'You'll get the dog?'

'Yes.'

'Oh, Daddy, thank you!'

Sonja tapped an elegantly shod foot on the floor. 'What about our dinner arrangements? I don't see that it's necessary for you to go, David. Can't you send someone else? Mr O'Connor would do just as well.'

'Terence is too old to go climbing up and down hills in the dark with a sick dog, Sonja,' he said with what Anne thought was commendable patience. 'We'll eat a little later, that's all.' He put down his drink and left the room, Jessica running along behind him and telling him all about the dog.

'So you've won this round, Miss Winters,' Sonja said in a brittle voice. 'Don't expect to win the next one.'

'I'm not sure I know what you mean,' Anne said carefully.

'You may have taken David from me for an hour or two —but I am the one who has him at night.'

There was no mistaking her meaning. Remembering the two bedrooms across the hall from each other, Anne felt herself flinch inwardly. So Sonja was David's mistress. It should come as no surprise to her; he had always been devastatingly attractive to women, nor was he the type to remain celibate for long. Why she should suddenly feel like crying, she had no idea.

'I'm going to get some dry socks,' she said flatly. 'Have a nice dinner.'

As she waited for David by the back door, she saw that it was nearly dark. She tucked her hair under the cap and laced up her boots again, then heard him say, 'Ready?'

He was wearing brown cords and a lumberman's jacket, with sealskin mukluks on his feet; he looked large, tough and resourceful. A flashlight swung from his hand. 'You'll have to show me the way,' he said.

'I hope I can find it again in the dark.'

'No doubt the dog will make enough noise that we won't have any problem,' was his dry response.

They set off down the hill, their footsteps crunching in the snow. A cloud cover had obscured the stars and the air was damp and heavy. 'Feels like snow's on the way,' David said impersonally.

There was a remoteness about him, a sense of more than the physical distance between them. Hurrying to keep up with his long strides, Anne said tentatively, 'I'm sorry we spoiled your arrangements for dinner.'

'That's all right. Jessica's more important than a dinner date and she was pretty upset about this dog. I suppose the next thing will be that she'll want to keep the wretched animal.'

Anne smothered a laugh. 'Wait until you see it—it's not what you'd call show dog material.'

'That's what I was afraid of.' His voice was warmer now and imperceptibly she felt herself relax. He swept the flashlight ahead of them. 'That looks like the best way to go—it's not as steep.'

He transferred the torch to his other hand and held out a hand to her. After a fractional hesitation she took it, and together they scrambled down the slippery bank; more than once his supporting arm kept her from falling. They came to a more level area, but he showed no inclination to drop her hand, so they walked along side by side.

The strangeness of the situation suddenly struck Anne, so that momentarily she stumbled. The thin yellow beam of the torch only served to emphasise the overwhelming solitude of their surroundings; to her ears came the murmur of the river as the black-shadowed trees crowded around them. Through the winter night she and David, her husband, were walking hand in hand ... the situation had a sense of rightness that profoundly disturbed her. It confronted her, not for the first time, with an unanswerable dilemma: how could the man who was so loving towards his daughter be the same man who had behaved with such unutterable cruelty to his wife? It was a mystery to Anne, a mystery that more and more strongly she wanted to solve. As they approached the riverbank, where the wind sighed through the trees, she realised with incredulity that she was happy—happy to be with David. Not watching where she was going, she tripped over a cake of ice, and would have fallen had he not grabbed her by the sleeve. As she fell against him and his arm came around her, it gave her a feeling of security that she knew she had been lacking for months. Yet how could that be? In the gold glow of light from the torch she stared up at him, her conflicting emotions mirrored in her expressive features—bewilderment, wonder, the fugitive gleam of happiness....

His face was very serious, his eyes impenetrable, although perhaps there was a questioning in their depths. 'What's the matter?' he asked. 'You look as though you've just seen a ghost.'

So she had—the ghost of a marriage. Unable to answer him, she found her gaze locked with his. 'You mystify me,' he said huskily. Then he bent his head and his lips met hers in a kiss of such tender warmth that she felt her bones melt in her body. Wordlessly she clung to him.

From the thicket came the mournful howling of a dog. Slowly David straightened, although for a long moment he held her chin in his hand, his eyes roaming over her face as though to memorise it. Then he said with a hint of reckless laughter in his voice, 'On with the rescue!' He glanced over his shoulder. 'I gather we're heading for that patch of woods?'

Anne nodded, quite unable to say a word. What was happening to her? The man whom she had just kissed was David, her husband—whom she hated. Yet in all honesty, she knew had he kissed her a second time, she would have welcomed it. . . .

The dog was barking now, a steady, deep-pitched baying. David went ahead of her, shining the torch over the tangle of trees. They made their way to the centre of the thicket, often bent almost double to avoid the snow-laden boughs. Finally David's torch came to rest on the dog in the trap. It was giving them a frenzied welcome, its pink tongue lolling out of its mouth.

'Good lord, it's huge!' David exclaimed, eyeing it more knowledgeably than Anne had. 'Looks like a cross between a Labrador retriever and a Newfoundland dog. Okay, fellow, quieten down now.'

There was an unmistakable note of authority in his voice and Anne was amused to see the dog subside on its haunches, although it still whined softly in its throat. David knelt beside it. 'Hold the flashlight, will you?' he asked, absently passing it to Anne. He broke off a couple of good-sized sticks from a nearby tree. 'When I open the trap, I want you to insert these in the angles. That way, it won't be able to shut again. Ready?'

'Yes.'

His teeth clenched with effort, the muscles in his hands and wrists taut, he levered the ugly steel jaws of the trap apart. 'Now!' he gasped. As she carefully inserted the pieces of wood, Anne realised David had freed the dog's paw, being as gentle as he could. 'We'll have to get him to the vet,' he muttered. 'It's a nasty wound, and there might be broken bones. If you go ahead with the torch, I'll carry him.' He cradled the shivering creature in his arms, where it gazed at him with such brown-eyed adoration that Anne had to swallow a tendency to giggle.

The trip up the hill was more arduous, and David was breathing heavily by the time they neared the house. 'Will you go ahead and tell Terence to bring the car round? We'll go straight to the vet's, I think.'

She did as she was told; as she approached the house, Jessica came catapulting out of the back door, and ran up to David. 'You got him! Isn't he beautiful?'

'Well, that's a matter of opinion. We're taking him to the vet, Jess, his foot is hurt.'

'Can I come?'

'I suppose so.'

So the four of them plus the dog bundled into the car and drove to a businesslike brick clinic about five miles east of Stornaway. The vet, a lanky young man with a thatch of vivid red hair, greeted David like a friend, then directed all his attention to the dog, getting David to carry it into his office while Anne and Jessica sat in the waiting room. Jessica soon grew tired of just sitting, so she and Anne went for a walk outside around the paddock and animal stalls that flanked the clinic. As they went back inside, the vet and David had just emerged, David carrying the dog, who now had his foreleg encased in thick bandages. As they drove home, David explained that the vet hadn't known of any missing dogs in the area.

'Can we keep him, Daddy?' came the inevitable question.

'I guess so,' David said in a resigned tone. 'I got him his rabies and distemper shots, figuring you'd ask that. You'd better give him a name.'

'Rover,' said Jessica without any hesitation.

'Oh, Jess, can't you think of something more original than that?' David groaned.

'That's a nice name! Anne read me a story about a dog called Rover.'

'It's all your fault,' David said, sending a grin in Anne's direction that did funny things to her heart. As they all trooped into the house, she could have been one of the family—and was visited by a sharp longing to be just that.

She paused at the kitchen door to help Jessica take off her boots; her glasses had steamed up in the warmth and without thinking she slipped them into her pocket.

'You've been gone all this time for that?' It was Sonja, her nose wrinkling fastidiously as she saw Rover.

Jessica sprang to his defence. 'He's beautiful!'

'We'd better fix him up a bed,' David said diplomatically. 'Deirdre, you must know where there's an old rug.'

Sonja's gaze travelled from the gaunt black creature lying on the floor to Jessica and Anne. Anne was still struggling with the zipper on the little girl's boots. Their two faces were close together, each flushed and bright-eyed, each identically heart-shaped; the caps they wore hid the difference in hair colouring.

For a moment Sonja's eyes went blank with shock, then they narrowed speculatively. It was at his moment that Anne chanced to look up, perhaps subconsciously aware of the other woman's regard. Their eyes met and clashed. There was no mistaking the message in Sonja's expression: she had seen the uncanny resemblance between Anne and Jessica, and was busy drawing her own conclusions.

Anne felt her nerves tighten with panic. She had already made an enemy in Sonja. How would the other woman use this new discovery? Not to Anne's advantage, of that she could be sure....

David came back into the kitchen carrying a woven basket and a frayed blue rug, both of which he arranged in the corner by the stove. Sonja opened her mouth to speak. Anne found herself frozen with fear, quite unable to do

anything to stop the other woman. Sonja said, her husky
voice caressing the word, 'David——'

'Yes?' He glanced up. Sonja was still wearing the cocktail dress, its soft chiffon folds swathing her voluptuous
figure, but her eyes, Anne thought dispassionately, were as
cold and hard as the diamonds she wore. When she spoke,
her words were such an anticlimax that Anne felt almost
dizzy with relief. 'You are going to keep that dog?'

'Yes, Sonja—at least, unless its owner turns up, which
seems doubtful after all this time. Jessica's been wanting a
dog for some time——' he eyed Rover philosophically,
'well, she's got one. Not quite what I had in mind, admittedly, but I wouldn't be surprised if he makes up in de-
votion what he lacks in breeding.'

Deirdre O'Connor came in with a dish of food, which
Rover demolished in a few swift gulps. 'Give him some
more in a couple of hours,' David suggested. 'The vet
warned against over-feeding at first.'

The dog then hobbled over to the bed, sniffed it all over,
circled a few times and collapsed with a theatrical sigh, his
nose on his paws. His tail gave a couple of thuds, as if he
sensed everyone's attention on him.

'I'll run up and change, Sonja, and then I'll meet you in
the study in five minutes. I don't think I finished that drink,
did I?' David gave Sonja an intimate smile, which somehow excluded everyone else in the room.

'I'll pour you a new one, just the way you like it. After
all, the night is yet young,' the blonde told him, running her
eyes suggestively over his lean body.

With bitter clarity, Anne knew this was all for her benefit. It was by no means coincidence that in just over five
minutes she found herself hovering in the hall outside the
half-open study door, having left Jessica in the kitchen with
Rover. From inside came the murmur of voices and Sonja's
husky laugh; it made Anne's hackles rise. Then her attention sharpened, for she heard Sonja say, 'David, I noticed
a most strange thing in the kitchen.'

'Oh? What was that?'

'Miss Winters had taken off her glasses when she came in the house and she was standing beside Jessica. David, they looked enough alike to be sisters—or mother and daughter. How could that be?'

There was an infinitesimal pause before David said smoothly, 'As a matter of fact, they are related—didn't I tell you?'

'No, you never told me that.' The voice sharp.

'Remiss of me,' David murmured. Anne's nails dug into her palms in an agony of suspense. 'Yes, they're distant cousins——'

'The resemblance is too great for that,' Sonja interrupted stridently.

'Not at all—heredity does some strange things. Marianne's side of the family has pretty well died out—she's an orphan herself—so I took pity on her and gave her the job. One should look after one's own, I believe.'

This last sentence struck Anne as the height of irony, even as her mind was deluged with questions. Why was David lying? He knew as well as she that there was no blood relationship between them. . . .

'It's quite like a novel,' Sonja said, unable to hide the sarcasm in her tone. 'The poor relation comes as the housekeeper.'

'Not everyone is born with all your advantages, Sonja.'

There was an instant's silence. 'Always you come to the defence of this girl, this mysterious Miss Winters who looks so like your daughter—why is that, David?'

Impatiently David said, 'You're making far too much out of nothing, Sonja. Do we have to spend the entire evening discussing Miss Winters, estimable though she no doubt is? Drink up, darling—I changed our reservations and we should get going if we're to make it on time.'

'Very well.' There was a rustle of chiffon. 'One kiss before we go, David——'

Her cheeks burning, Anne fled to her room. God, what a mess she'd landed herself in! Loving Jessica as she did, she knew it would destroy her to have to leave the child.

But she couldn't stay indefinitely under false pretences, for the situation was becoming more and more complicated. Sonja, she was sure, wanted to marry David—and how wrong that would be for Jessica, for the woman had made no secret of her dislike for children. And it would be wrong for David, too, Anne thought painfully. Only too well she knew how passionate and loving a man he could be. Sonja was not like that—she was cold and calculating, essentially only interested in Sonja. She would stifle David's innate warmth and generosity. Perhaps she already had, Anne thought drearily, remembering how harshly David had treated her, Anne, on more than one occasion. Full circle, her mind came back to that one unanswerable question: why had David lied to Sonja? Distant cousins—it was nonsense!

Her head was beginning to ache. She hung up her outdoor clothes, firmly planted her glasses on her nose and went downstairs to get Jessica, for it was past her bedtime.

Twice more during the evening Anne fed Rover small portions of the leftover stew Deirdre had produced; it would take a while to get him back in shape, she knew, looking at the outline of his ribs under the stark fur. Perhaps tomorrow she could give him a good brushing. And she and Jess had better go to the store and buy some dog-food before he got too accustomed to eating beef stew!

She went to her room around eleven. David and Sonja were not back yet, and as she lay on the bed trying to read, she knew she was straining to hear the sound of the car. She must have fallen into a light sleep, for the next thing she heard was footsteps on the stairs, then David's deep voice murmuring something, and Sonja's answering laugh.

Anne sat up, feeling fingers of desolation curl around her heart. Without stopping to think she switched off the light, then eased her door open. She could discern the two figures in the hall; standing very close together, they were talking in low, intimate tones. As Anne's eyes became adjusted to the dark, she saw that Sonja was toying with the lapels on David's jacket. Then with deliberate provocativeness Sonja

moved her body against David's and with her long, white
fingers pulled his head down to hers. The two figures became one ... the kiss seemed to go on for ever, until Anne
could bear it no longer. She retreated into her own room
and began to close the door with infinite care; it would be
utterly humiliating for the couple in the hall to know that
she had been watching them. But as she did so, she heard
David say something and Sonja respond, although their
voices were too low for her to distinguish the words. Then
she heard a decisive click as one—only one—of the two
bedroom doors down the hall was closed. Silence fell.

The conclusion was inescapable: David and Sonja had
gone into the same room. Anne collapsed on to her bed, the
back of her hand pressed against her mouth, her eyes agon-
ised as they stared sightlessly into the darkness. A yawning
pit had opened before her, and helpless to prevent herself
she fell into its depths, there to be overwhelmed by the
demons of jealousy. A pain that was actually physical
doubled her over, as again and again the words beat at her
drooping head—David and Sonja ... David and Sonja ...
she could not cry, for the torment was too cruel to be eased
by tears.

Afterwards, she had no idea how much time had passed.
She slowly straightened into a sitting position. Her body
was sore all over, as though she had been flailed; she felt
desperately tired. But she had emerged with her mind
working with a crystal clarity.

She loved David, she thought numbly. Perhaps she had
never stopped loving him. All her protestations of hatred,
all her fears of getting in touch with him again—these had
been masks, which had hidden the truth from her. She
loved him ... and would love him until the day she died.

He did not, however, love her. Jessica was the bitter
proof of that. Four years ago he had deliberately lied to
Anne, thereby depriving her of her own daughter. That action could not be construed as anything but sadistic, moti-
vated by a hatred and contempt so all-consuming that even
now it could make Anne shudder. No, David had no love

for his ex-wife. Whether or not he loved Sonja, Anne couldn't say, although certainly he was sleeping with her. They were lovers—she did not see how she could bear this knowledge. Equally, she knew she had no choice. For Jessica's sake she was trapped at Stornaway, trapped in a situation that could do nothing but destroy her by degrees.

When she went downstairs the next morning, she had done her best to hide the ravages of a sleepless night. All too soon it was made plain that she had not succeeded. When she carried her breakfast into the alcove, David was there before her, reading the newspaper and sipping a second cup of coffee.

'Good morning, Marianne,' he said, with that slight stress on her name that always made her feel uncomfortable. 'What's wrong—are you ill?'

'No, of course not.' He, she noticed bleakly, looked perfectly at ease, his blue eyes guileless, his shapely fingers curved around his coffee cup. She thought of these hands on Sonja's body and felt herself wince.

'You look like death warmed up,' he drawled.

'Thanks,' she said sarcastically, looking down at the two pieces of toast which she now realised she could not possibly force herself to eat.

'Do you have a fever? There's a bad 'flu bug on the go——'

'I am not ill,' she said clearly. 'Now will you please leave me alone?'

'Unfortunately, you're not in the position for giving the orders here, my dear.'

She looked up, feeling her stomach quiver with apprehension. His air of relaxation had vanished: he was as taut as a lion about to pounce—and just as dangerous. 'I make the decisions around here,' he reiterated softly. 'Maybe you aren't ill, but you're certainly overtired. Terence will drive you to the airport today and you can get a flight to Halifax; he'll check for reservations before you leave. You have some days off coming to you, and by the look of you a rest won't do you any harm. What's today—Thursday? As long as you're back by Monday, that'll be all right.'

Anne was bereft of speech. Her vision had narrowed to a pair of pitiless blue eyes. He was sending her away—he couldn't do that, he couldn't! 'No,' she stammered, 'please, no—I don't want to go.'

'You're not being given any choice. I've said you're going and you'll go.'

'You can't make me——'

'I certainly can. Don't look so distraught, I'm not firing you. I've said you can come back on Monday. That is, if you don't decide to stay in Halifax yith your friend Jonathan.'

She disregarded this. 'Jessica will miss me.'

'No doubt. But as I've said before, I don't want Jessica getting too dependent on you.'

'Why not?' she burst out, throwing discretion to the winds.

He raised a disdainful eyebrow. 'I would have thought it was obvious. You seem to be enjoying it here at the moment, but no beautiful young woman like you is going to bury herself in the country indefinitely.'

Anne opened her mouth to protest, but he forestalled her. 'Spare your breath. If there's one thing I've learned in life, it's that women are not to be trusted. Here today and gone tomorrow, if you'll pardon the triteness of the phrase. I can't imagine that you're any different from the rest. I'm merely ensuring that Jessica will not be overly hurt when you do leave us.'

'Jessica loves me already,' Anne said quietly, grey eyes stormy in her white face.

'Be careful how you use that word "love". It's the most misused word in the language,' David said harshly. 'There'll be no more discussion, Miss Winters. My mind is made up. You'll leave today and unless I hear to the contrary, I'll expect you back on the Monday morning flight.'

'You're nothing but a dictator!' she raged. 'You have no right to arrange my life for me. "Go to Halifax, Miss Winters." What happens if I don't want to go to Halifax?'

'I trust you won't let your Jonathan hear you talking like that——'

'He's not "my" Jonathan!'

He pushed back his chair, glaring at her so fiercely that she shrank back. The sun gleamed on his tawny hair. 'Frankly, I don't give a damn if you go to Timbuctoo. Just get out of my sight for the next three days.' So he could be alone with Sonja, she thought bleakly. 'Do you hear?'

'I could hardly fail to.'

'If Jessica spoke to me like that, I'd give her a good spanking,' he grated, his body looming over her.

'Well, I'm not Jessica, and you're not my father,' she retorted.

'I've never had any aspirations to be your father, Marianne Winters—and you can interpret that any way you like. And now I'll go and make the arrangements with Terence. Kindly be ready at whatever time he says, and leave him a phone number where you can be reached.'

She was beyond the point of curbing her tongue. 'I'll leave him the number of Jonathan's apartment,' she said sweetly. 'You can always reach me there.'

'You little bitch!'

'What a marvellous double standard you have!' she blazed. 'It's fine to condemn me for staying at Jonathan's— but the fact that Sonja is your mistress is another story altogether.'

'Whether Sonja is or is not my mistress need hardly concern you.'

He was right, of course—why had she ever started this? Rigid with mingled mortification and rage, she felt two spots of colour burning in her cheeks, she felt her eyes fall before his.

'Goodbye, Miss Winters. Do have a pleasant holiday,' he said viciously.

He came round her side of the table. Seizing her chin, he roughly jerked it upwards. His kiss was brief and brutal. Before she could say a word, he had left the room.

Anne sat limply in her chair, wanting nothing more than

to put her head down on the table and cry her eyes out. But no doubt Jessica would be down for breakfast very shortly, so she couldn't do that. The morning sun streamed through the windows, mocking her, as bright and uncaring as Sonja's diamonds. It seemed as though even the weather was in league with David, she thought bitterly, for it was a perfect day for flying. She'd better go and pack.

She got up, but instead of leaving the room was drawn to the windows that overlooked the bay. Under a pale morning sky the hills lay softly rounded by the blanket of snow. Dark, spiky spruces clustered in the valleys. It was a world of dazzling whiteness with an austere and lonely beauty ... down in the valley by the river she could see the thicket where they had found Rover and where only last night she and David had walked hand in hand, and he had kissed her with warmth and tenderness. The contrast with his behaviour this morning was so great that in spite of herself, tears crowded her eyes.

CHAPTER SEVEN

THE morning passed, outwardly much like any other. Terence reported that he had obtained a reservation on the three-twenty flight so they would leave the house about two. Anne and Jessica walked to the small general store to buy dog food, and while they were gone Anne broached the subject of her trip.

'Your father's given me three days off, Jess, and he's booked me a flight to Halifax. He says I look tired and need a rest.'

Jessica looked at Anne earnestly, her little nose wrinkled so endearingly that Anne's heart lurched with tenderness. 'You've got purple under your eyes!' she announced with an air of triumph.

'Thanks, chum!'

'But you'll come back?' Jessica asked in sudden anxiety.

'Yes, dear, I promise. I'll be back on Monday.'

'Well, I'll have Rover to play with,' said Jessica philosophically, and Anne was relieved that Jessica's insecurity had been so easily allayed. At least Jessica trusted her—even if David didn't.

While Jessica had a nap after lunch, Anne packed a few things in her case; earlier she had phoned Jonathan at the gallery and had been somewhat cheered by his pleasure at the prospect of a visit from her. He would be meeting her at the Halifax airport.

A light tap came at her door. 'Come in.'

In a wave of expensive perfume Sonja entered, closing the door behind her. As usual she was exquisitely dressed, this time in a rose pink dress of supple suede, a silk scarf tucked in the neckline. Her hair was elaborately coiled around her ears, where pale pink opals glistened. Anne immediately felt dull and dowdy in her grey slacks and matching sweater, knowing that Sonja would be sure to notice the dark circles under her eyes.

Without preamble Sonja said, 'So you're leaving?'

'Only for a few days. I'll be back on Monday.'

'Yes?'

Anne forced herself to meet the other woman's eyes. 'Yes.'

'I think it would be better for you if you did not return.'

'Why, Sonja?'

'Because I might be tempted to make life very unpleasant for you.'

You've already done that, Anne thought silently, although the last thing she wanted to do was give the woman the satisfaction of knowing it. 'And just how do you propose to do that?' she said steadily.

'By putting an end to this foolish pretence of yours. Marianne Winters—bah! You're no more a distant cousin of David's than I am.'

'You're quite wrong. My name *is* Marianne Winters—I have papers to prove it. Do you think David would have hired me as a companion for Jessica without checking up on my references?'

'I don't know how you fooled him, but you don't fool me. When I saw you and Jessica together yesterday—I knew. Yes, Anne Metcalfe, I knew.'

Not by the slightest move did Anne betray her consternation. She said impatiently, 'Look, I don't know what you're getting at and I don't really care. I'd prefer you to go—I have packing to do.'

'I would advise you to pack everything. Because I intend to tell David the truth. You may have presented yourself as his long-lost cousin'—Anne stifled an hysterical giggle— 'but I know you are his wife—and the mother of Jessica.'

'You're crazy,' Anne said shortly, turning away to get a shirt from her cupboard.

'No, I'm not crazy. I think you're the crazy one to have come back. Whatever did you hope to gain?'

There was genuine curiosity in Sonja's voice; Sonja,

Anne knew, would never expose herself to hurt and humiliation for the sake of a child. 'Exactly, Miss Sorenson,' she replied. 'Why would David's wife come back, particularly as an impostor? There's no possible reason. You've proved my point—I'm Marianne Winters.'

'No!' Sonja hissed. 'You're Anne Metcalfe. You can't be otherwise, looking as you do. I'm going to tell David you're his wife.' She paused suggestively. 'He'll be pleased, you know.'

'Pleased?' echoed Anne, both shocked and delighted by Sonja's statement. Her pleasure was short-lived.

'Why, yes. You see, he's wanted to divorce you for some time now. But how could he, when he did not know where you were. Oh, I'm sure he could have found out eventually by hiring lawyers and tracing you that way, but it would have been time-consuming and costly. You've solved the problem very nicely.'

Dumbstruck, Anne wondered if Sonja was telling the truth—did David want to divorce her? 'Why, after all this time, would he suddenly want a divorce?'

'To marry me, of course. I thought I'd made that clear.'

'What about Jessica?' said Anne in a thin voice that, had she but known it, betrayed her completely.

'What about her?' Sonja drawled, examining her fingernails with an air of faint boredom.

'You don't love Jessica!'

'That's true enough. It's David I'm interested in, not Jessica.' Maliciously Sonja added, 'I will have to keep you on as a housekeeper, will I not?'

'You don't even love David.'

'All this foolish talk about love! David is rich, handsome, cultured—and I mean to have him. Don't make any mistake about that. Neither you, nor anyone else, Jessica included, will stand in my way.'

Fiercely Anne cried, 'You talk of him as though he's a possession, a thing—he's a man, a flesh-and-blood man with joys and sorrows and needs—a passionate, loving man. How can you be so cold-blooded?'

Sonja laughed, a clear bell-like sound that chilled Anne to the bone. 'You give yourself away with every word, you know.' Her pale eyes narrowed with calculation. 'I do believe you still love him—is that why you came back? I shall have to tell him that as well, shan't I? How amused he'll be!'

'Don't!' The word was torn from Anne. Too late, she realised everything she had admitted by that one short word.

'Let's strike a bargain, then. I won't tell him you are still in love with him. In return, you won't come back from Halifax. That's fair enough, isn't it?'

'It's monstrously unfair,' Anne whispered. 'I promised Jessica I'd come back—how can I go back on that promise?'

'That's your problem, not mine.' The blonde woman moved purposely towards the door. 'At least this way you'll avoid a face-to-face confrontation with your ex-husband and the divorce can be dealt with in a civilised manner.'

'I'm not sure there's anything civilised about a divorce,' said Anne coldly.

'That's because you persist in wallowing in sentimentality. David and I are not like that—we are sophisticated enough to know that life is a matter of compromises.'

'If David is like that now, then *you* have changed him. He wasn't like that with me.'

'Be quiet!' Sonja demanded.

Anne could not help being pleased that she had finally punctured the other woman's icy composure. 'Even if he's like that with you, he loves Jessica.' She leaned forward for emphasis, her voice quivering with feeling. 'Be his mistress if you want, Sonja—but I beg you, don't marry him. Jessica needs a mother, a loving mother who cares for her. Please don't deprive her of that——'

'David and I will marry,' Sonja snapped, her voice high-pitched with temper. 'You can't stop us! So for the sake of your pride don't come back here, Anne Metcalfe. Not unless you want to be humiliated and hurt in front of David and in front of your precious Jessica. I warn you—don't come back.' She turned and went out, shutting the door sharply behind her.

Anne shoved some more clothes in her suitcase and banged it shut. She had twenty minutes to get ready. Defiantly she chose a flattering flared skirt and velvet blazer from the back of her cupboard, teaming them with a silk blouse and tight-fitting leather boots. She brushed her hair into a smooth roll on the back of her head. After recklessly applying make-up, she added gold hoop earrings and an extravagant splash of her favourite perfume. To hell with all of them, she fumed, surveying with considerable satisfaction the immaculately groomed young woman in the mirror. Dark glasses added an intriguing air of mystery. Her chin held high, she picked up her case and stalked out of her room.

She was halfway down the stairs, although she had not yet caught sight of David waiting by the front door, when a shrill voice piped, 'Wait, Anne! Wait for me.'

Jessica caught up with her, with Pooh Bear dragging behind. She stared up at Anne, wide-eyed. 'You look nice,' she said gravely. 'You're pretty.'

Deeply touched, Anne said, 'Thank you, Jessica.' They continued down the stairs together, Anne accommodating herself to Jessica's short legs. Then she stopped short. David was standing at the foot of the stairs, a briefcase in his hand, his camelhair coat flung over one arm.

'Where are you going?' Anne demanded, thrown off balance by his unexpected appearance.

'I'm going into Charlottetown with you,' he said, raising a sardonic eyebrow at her gaucheness. 'Once I've dropped you at the airport, I have some business to attend to.' He looked at his watch. 'Are you ready?'

Her heart sank and all her newfound bravado deserted her. An hour alone in the car with David was more than she could handle.

' 'Bye, Anne,' said Jessica in a little voice, clutching Pooh Bear more firmly.

Momentarily Anne forgot her own troubles. She bent

down and kissed Jessica's cheek. ''Bye, darling.' Knowing she had no choice in the matter, she added, 'I'll see you on Monday. Be a good girl, won't you, and take care of Rover.'

Gently she released herself from Jessica's clinging fingers, trying not to see how forlorn the child looked. 'I'm ready,' she said to David.

But he too was looking at his daughter. 'Do you want to come to Charlottetown with us, Jess?'

'Oh, yes!'

'Terence could take you for an ice cream while I go to the bank,' he told her.

'Chocolate on the bottom and strawberry on top?'

David gave a comical grimace. 'Anything you like.'

Warmed by his concern for Jessica, Anne found the child's coat and boots in the hall closet and helped her into them. Then they all left the house together. The drive to Charlottetown was accomplished in relative silence, since Jessica seemed content to sit between Anne and David, her usual flow of chatter lessened by the unexpected treat. But as they approached the airport buildings, she piped up, 'What are you going to do in Halifax, Anne?'

'I haven't really thought about it,' Anne hedged. 'I expect I'll visit some of my friends from the hospital where I used to work.'

'Will you see your boy-friend?' the little girl asked artlessly.

'You mean Jonathan? He's not really my boy-friend, Jess,' said Anne, uncomfortably aware of David sitting silently in the corner. 'But I will be seeing him. He's meeting my plane in Halifax.'

'Did you leave a phone number with Terence?' David asked, his voice cold and incisive.

'Yes.' Some demon of mischief prompted her to add, 'I left the number at the gallery as well as Jonathan's apartment. So you should be able to reach me day or night.' She had no intention of staying at Jonathan's apartment, and had already asked him to book her a motel room, but David did not need to know that.

'How very convenient,' he lashed back, his blue eyes flashing with some undecipherable emotion.

Already ashamed of herself, she was about to tell him the truth when Jessica exclaimed, 'We're here! Look at the plane—is that yours, Anne?'

'Let's go and find out,' David said easily, and the moment passed.

Anne checked her suitcase and picked up her ticket at the counter. Jessica had already run to the window that overlooked the runway, and was standing there with her nose pressed against the glass. As Anne watched her, David said, 'Either Terence or I will meet your flight on Monday morning.'

'Thank you.' What else could she say?

'You will come back, Miss Winters?' He spoke with an undertone of menace.

'I've said I will.' Unconsciously her eyes flew to Jessica's figure by the window.

He said savagely, 'Since you make it so obvious that Jessica is your only interest, I shall ensure that if you don't come back on Monday, you won't see her again.'

Anne blanched at the total unexpectedness of this attack, ignorant of how she could have offended him. 'Are you threatening me?' she said slowly.

David had never looked more arrogant, more sure of himself. 'Yes, I do believe I am.'

'I—I don't understand,' she faltered. A group of passengers brushed against her so that she had to move closer to David.

'I only want to make sure you come back.' He bit the words off, his face inscrutable.

Bewildered, she felt as though he was playing with her, as a cat torments its prey. She was gathering her courage to ask him why he wanted her back, when the bored voice of the announcer came across the loudspeaker. 'Air Canada Flight 235 to Halifax now boarding at the main gate. All aboard, no smoking, please.'

David called Jessica and the little girl came running.

'They put gas in your plane. It's got red paint on the tail. Will you wave at me from the steps?'

It was impossible for Anne not to laugh. 'Yes, I will.' She gave the child a brief hug. 'See you soon.'

As she straightened, all the love she bore for her daughter was still shining in her face. She looked straight into David's eyes, so blue and penetrating, and was desperately aware of the magnetic pull of his attraction. His hands fell hard on her shoulders. He bent his head and kissed her so thoroughly that when he finally released her her cheeks were pink, her eyes a vivid green. Surely he must hear the frantic pounding of her heart. 'You'll miss the plane if you stand there too long,' he mocked.

'Oh, you're impossible!' she spluttered, and began to hurry after the other passengers, fumbling for her boarding pass. At the top of the steps before entering the plane, she remembered to wave to Jessica. The child waved back. David did not.

The flight to Halifax seemed all too brief; there was not enough time for her to make the transition from David and Jessica to Jonathan. As the plane came in to land, she looked out of the window at a bleak and wintry landscape very different from the open fields and rounded hills of the Island. Here the ground was rough and rock-strewn, the spruce trees stunted by poor soil. From the air she could see the dark ribbons of the highway. The ground rushed up to meet them and the plane bumped twice as they landed.

Jonathan was waiting for her just inside the big doors of the airport terminal. He kissed her, then for a minute held her away from him, his pleasant brown eyes concerned. 'You do look as though you need a rest,' he told her.

'Do I look that bad?'

'Stop fishing for compliments, Anne. You're gorgeous and you know it!'

She laughed, nuzzling her face into his collar in a gesture of affection. 'I had to work hard for that one, didn't I? But I am tired, actually.'

'Well, I'm taking you to my apartment where you're go-

ing to sit with your feet up while I cook dinner. I'll even
let you off washing the dishes afterwards—how's that?'

Jonathan was something of a gourmet cook, as she well
knew; but far more than by the prospect of a good meal,
she was touched by his solicitude towards her. After David's
battering of her emotions, Jonathan's kindness was balm to
her senses. 'Sounds wonderful,' she said gratefully. 'You're
too good to me, Jon.'

'Nonsense,' he said gruffly. 'Look, the baggage is arriving. Let's get your case and go home.'

After a pleasant and relaxing evening, Anne was in her
motel by eleven o'clock and slept the clock around. Jonathan had business commitments all day Friday, so she
visited hospital friends, shopped, and met Jonathan for a
drink at a pub by the waterfront later in the evening. On
Saturday they left Halifax early in the morning and drove
through the Annapolis valley, then down to the south
shore, visiting several resident artists on their way; they
didn't get back to the apartment until after six.

Although Anne had enjoyed driving through the countryside and meeting new people, she had been conscious all
day of an undercurrent of tension, that had built up to a
level of acute anxiety by the time they reached Halifax
again. Although she had inwardly chided herself for feeling
like that for no known cause, she had not been able to
dissipate her uneasiness.

'Anything wrong?' Jonathan had asked, with his usual
sensitivity to her moods.

'Nothing I can put a name to,' she said as they walked
into his apartment block. 'I just feel anxious, upset—as
though something's badly wrong.' She gave herself a shake.
'It's silly! Talk about female megrims!'

Jonathan was mixing them a cocktail while Anne investi-
gated the contents of the refrigerator, when the telephone
rang. He put down the cocktail shaker and went into the
den to answer it. When he came back a minute later, his
face was serious. 'It's for you—it's David.'

'David?' she repeated foolishly. 'Where is he? Is he all
right?'

'At Stornaway. I guess he's okay, although he sounded pretty abrupt. I don't know him very well, but I'd say he's upset about something. You'd better go and speak to him.'

It seemed as though her forebodings were to be justified. She walked through the hall to the den, where Jonathan kept his collection of prints and Eskimo sculpture. The telephone was on the desk; she eyed it as though it were a rattlesnake. Sonja must have carried out her threat to tell David about the presence of his ex-wife under his own roof....

She picked up the receiver. 'Hello?' she said, her voice a thin thread.

'Anne?'

Her heart sank. So the game was over ... 'Yes?'

'Jessica's ill and she's asking for you. Can you come back?'

Jessica was ill—all other considerations fled from her mind. She sank into the chair by the desk, for her legs had turned to water. 'Of course I can. But David, what's wrong with her? Is she seriously ill?' Engulfed by a paralysing fear, she waited for his reply, her palm damp on the receiver.

'She came down with a fever yesterday—headache, sore throat, vomiting. She was worse this morning, so I got the doctor. He says she's got a bad dose of the 'flu that's going around. She's on antibiotics, and the doctor assures me that she'll be okay—she's not ill enough to be in hospital.' Anne could sense the worry and concern underlying his clipped phrases. 'But she's still feverish, and she keeps asking for you. I told her I'd phone you—I've been trying to reach you all day.'

'We went out early this morning and we only just got back. If only I'd known, I'd never have gone. Oh, David, of course I'll come——'

'I knew I could depend on you.' There was an odd undertone in his voice, but she did not stop to analyse it. 'There's a flight at eight-thirty—can you be on it?'

'Yes.'

'Good girl.' Her heart warmed at these simple words of

praise. 'I'll probably stay here with Jess, so Terence will meet you. And I'll tell Jessica you're coming. Thanks, Anne.'

The connection was cut. She put the phone down, conscious of one overriding need: to be at Jessica's side as soon as possible.

'What's up?' It was Jonathan.

'Jessica's ill. I have to go home, Jonathan.'

He grimaced with unaccustomed bitterness. 'So it's home, is it?'

She frowned at him, not really realising what she had said. 'What do you mean?'

'Stornaway—where David is—is home to you.'

'Stornaway is where Jessica is,' she said sharply. 'And she's ill—I have to go, Jonathan, surely you can see that?'

He ran his fingers through his hair, suddenly looking ten years older. 'I can see more than that, Anne,' he said wearily. 'You're back where you were four years ago, caught up with a man who doesn't care for you, who uses you when it's convenient for him——'

She paled, with painful honesty recognising the truth of his words. 'But——'

'You don't have to say anything more. Just by looking at you, I can tell I'm right. God, Anne, why did you ever go back there? You can't say I didn't warn you!'

With a touch of wry humour she remarked, 'I'm not saying anything of the kind. Oh, Jonathan, I know you warned me, and everything you've said is true, but right now that doesn't matter.' In an agony of impatience she swept on, 'Jessica is ill—she needs me. I'll have to get my case from the motel and get to the airport. What's the time?'

'Quarter to seven.'

'Please—will you drive me out there?'

He sighed heavily. 'You know I will.'

It was not until they were in the car and leaving the outskirts of the city that Anne found the courage to say something that she knew had to be said, for the sake of her own peace of mind. 'Jonathan,' she began, 'I need to talk to you.'

She rested an apologetic hand on his knee, gazing into his shadowed face. 'Before I went to the Island, you asked me to marry you. . . .' He said nothing, so she laboured on. 'Maybe since then you've changed your mind or met someone else——'

'No, Anne,' he said with heavy patience, 'I haven't met anyone else and I haven't changed my mind.'

'Everything you said earlier is true, I'm afraid. Stornaway is home to me. I love Jessica, and——' she shifted her gaze to her hands, clenched in her lap, 'I guess I never stopped loving David. I thought I hated him. I still hate what he did to me. I don't know how he could have been so cruel——'

'How can you love a man like that?'

'I don't know, Jonathan,' she said drearily. 'Love's never been known for its logic, has it? It would probably be much better for me if I could fall in love with you—you're kind and considerate, I know you'd be good to me. But I can't, Jonathan. I'm sorry—I just can't.'

The black highway streamed past them, the headlights of the oncoming cars a gold necklace in the dark. 'Maybe I wouldn't mind so much if I thought there was a chance for you to be happy with David, Anne,' Jonathan said finally. 'But all I can see is that you're heading deeper and deeper into trouble. For situations like yours, there aren't any happy endings.'

He was only confirming all her own fears. 'I know,' she said in a low voice. 'But I'm trapped, Jonathan. Because of Jessica, I'm trapped.'

Piercing the night, the bright beam of the searchlight on the control tower swung towards them; they were nearly there. Apart from her longing to be on the plane heading for the Island, Anne was glad that the drive was almost over. She felt desperately sorry for Jonathan, knowing all too well the pains of unrequited love, although she knew she had done the right thing to speak to him. To have encouraged him in any way, or to have given him false hopes for the future, would have been wrong.

Just before she boarded the plane he gave her a brief, hard kiss. His brown eyes deeply serious, he said, 'You know where I am if you need me. Don't hesitate to get in touch when—if anything goes wrong.'

She blinked back tears. 'I'm sorry things have worked out this way, Jonathan. I've hurt you, and I didn't mean to do that.'

His expression was wry. 'Luck of the game, I guess. Take care of yourself, Anne, and keep in touch.'

'Goodbye.' When she turned back to wave to him, he had already gone. As she entered the plane, she found her regrets for Jonathan crowded out of her mind by concern for Jessica. David would not have phoned if matters hadn't been serious—he was not the kind of man to easily ask a favour of anyone. To think that he had been trying to reach her all day. She could have been at Stornaway hours ago if only she'd known ... if only she'd trusted in that strange intuition she'd had that something was wrong....

Her first question to Terence was, 'How's Jessica?'

He heaved her case into the trunk. 'Once her father told her you were coming, she seemed a little better. But then her temperature climbed again just before I left. I'm glad you're back, miss. I don't think Mr Metcalfe slept a wink last night. The wee girl is the apple of his eye, and I know he's right worried.'

The black Mercedes ate up the miles and Anne found time to give thanks for the surprisingly mild weather. She could imagine only too well how she would have felt if a snowstorm had prevented her from leaving Halifax. In a surprisingly short time they were descending the hill towards Stornaway, where the lights of the house twinkled a welcome; they had become the lights of home, Anne knew. What was that phrase? Home is where the heart is. Like most clichés, it was only too true.

She hurried into the house, leaving Terence to cope with her luggage, and ran up the stairs. As she rounded the corner, she cannoned into a man's hard body—David's. All the breath was knocked from her lungs and she clung to him convulsively, intensely aware that his arms had come around her. She raised her face, her eyes shadowed with fear, an unspoken question in them.

'She's asleep. The doctor dropped in again an hour or so ago, and said to call him if she should get worse.' His eyes bored into hers. 'I'm glad you're here—thank you for coming back.'

His quiet words touched her to the heart. 'I couldn't do anything else,' she said honestly.

He took her by the hand. 'Come and have a look at her.'

They entered the bedroom together. Jessica was still sleeping, but her cheeks were hectically flushed and her little body was restless under the covers. Pooh Bear was sprawled on the pillow. As Anne and David stood there, Anne was again visited by that sense of rightness: she belonged here with David and Jessica. If only she could always stay with them. . . .

When they were out in the hallway again, she said to David, 'Why don't you go and lie down for a while? You look terribly tired. I'll get changed, and then I'll go and sit with her.'

'You'll wake me if she should get worse?'

'Yes, of course.'

He stifled a yawn. 'Maybe I will try and sleep. I don't think I got much last night.' He patted her shoulder absently. 'Thanks.'

The hours passed slowly. Jessica woke and although she was pathetically pleased to see Anne, she soon subsided into a fretful delirium; Anne was glad of her nursing skills as she bathed the child's overheated body, gave her the pills the doctor had prescribed, and did all she could to make her more comfortable. By the time Jessica fell asleep again it was past midnight. Anne went to her room and changed into a long caftan-like robe, wishing she had thought to ask Terence for a folding cot which she could have put up in Jessica's room. For over an hour she sat quietly by the child's bed, pleased to see that the fever had dropped and Jessica's sleep seemed to be the normal sleep of a healthy child. The crisis appeared to be over.

There was a movement by the door and she gave a start

of surprise before she realised it was David. He walked in quietly, belting a dark blue robe about his waist. Going to the bed, he lightly touched Jessica's forehead and Anne saw the deep relief that spread over his face. He stood there for a minute looking down at his daughter, an expression of such unguarded tenderness in his face that Anne was moved almost to tears. Then he beckoned her to follow him, and they left the room together. 'She looks much better', he said.

'Mmm—I think she'll be all right now.'

He grinned at her lightheartedly, the lines of care gone from his face. 'What's the time?'

'Would you believe one-thirty?'

He yawned and stretched, the muscles rippling under his skin, bared by the open neckline of his robe.

'I'm starving,' he announced. 'Let's raid the refrigerator.'

'Now?'

'Sure—why not? Deirdre'll be mad at us tomorrow, but it'll be worth it.'

Anne chuckled. 'Okay!'

He grabbed her hand and pulled her down the hall; laughing like two children, they went downstairs and sneaked into the kitchen. From his bed by the stove, Rover wagged his tail. Anne knelt beside him, patting his domed head. 'He looks much better,' she marvelled.

'Wonderful what a square meal will do, isn't it? Talking of which, do you want a turkey sandwich and a piece of apple pie? Why don't you put the kettle on?'

She did as she was bid, moving with unstudied grace across the kitchen, her caftan swinging against her hips and the slender length of her legs. As she turned on the oven to heat the pastry, she said hopefully, 'We could whip some cream to go with the pie.'

'Good idea.' David got a tray from behind the refrigerator. 'Maybe we'd better eat upstairs, just in case Jessica should wake.'

'All right.' She smiled at him, an uncomplicated smile of pleasure, for she was seeing a side to David that she had thought was gone for ever—a boyish exuberance and sense of fun that she well remembered. As they prepared the meal, she rejoiced in their companionship; it was all the more precious in contrast to some of the bitter conflicts they had had.

'Have we got everything?' he asked.

She looked at the loaded tray. 'I should hope so. We'll be up half the night if we eat all that!'

'Nonsense, it'll make you sleep like a baby.'

They went upstairs and Anne said unselfconsciously, 'Why don't we go into my room? That way we'll be sure to hear Jessica.' She flipped on the bedside light and drew the curtains while David put down the tray. Perching on the end of the bed, she said, 'Pass me a sandwich, please.'

They ate in amicable silence, until eventually Anne said, 'I'm full! Deirdre makes terrific pies, doesn't she?'

'Yeah—the only trouble is, I think it was intended for tomorrow's lunch.' David went to the dresser to get a serviette at the same moment that she got up for her tea. Midway they nearly collided, and she was so relaxed that she merely smiled at him, all her defences down.

He stroked a strand of hair back from her face. 'I'm glad you came back.'

'So am I.'

It seemed the most natural thing in the world that he should slide his hands up her arms and bend his head to hers. His kiss began gently, his mouth tender and questing. He must have sensed the pliancy of her body in his arms, for the kiss deepened and became more demanding. Her lips parted under his.

Every nerve she possessed leaped into life at his touch; she ached with a sudden, passionate need for him. Her fingers parted his robe, sliding over the smooth arch of his ribs, tangling themselves in the hair on his chest. He strained her closer to him so that the heat of his body seemed to scorch her through the thin fabric of the caftan. His hands moulded her spine and caressed the curves of her hips and waist.

He swung her into his arms and laid her on the bed, turning off the lamp so the room was plunged into semi-darkness. Then his body fell across hers and she knew his urgency and desire were as great as her own. He found the zipper at the neck of her caftan and in one swift movement pulled it down to her waist, so that her skin gleamed palely.

'God, you're beautiful,' he exulted.

She ran her fingers through his hair and pulled his head down, drinking the fire of his kiss. Then he freed his mouth, sliding it down the whiteness of her neck, nibbling the softness of her shoulder. She gasped with delight as his fingers and mouth both found the roundness of her breast. Her nipple hardened instinctively. She was pierced by a pleasure that demanded fulfilment.

His taut thigh came between her legs and her hips moved sinuously in open invitation. On the tip of her tongue were those all-revealing words, 'I love you. . . .'

From the adjoining room a tiny voice called, 'Daddy! Daddy?'

Anne froze to stillness, with all her maternal instincts knowing Jessica must come first. David rolled off her and she saw him fastening his robe. 'Maybe you'd better come too,' he said in a low voice.

She hastily pulled up her zipper, then followed him down the hall, her eyes lingering lovingly on the strong column of his neck and the breadth of his shoulders. She was trying to restore some order to her tumbled hair as they entered Jessica's room. In the dim glow of the night-light, they could see that the little girl was not even awake; she must have cried out in her sleep. Anne straightened the covers, her silky hair falling forward, then felt Jessica's forehead: it was cool to the touch. 'We should really wake her to take another of those antibiotic pills—she ought to have one every six hours.'

Between them they roused Jessica enough to swallow a capsule, although she was asleep again by the time her head hit the pillow. Then Anne preceded David from the room. In the hall he turned her to face him. 'I think we'd better say goodnight,' he murmured, a glint of laughter in his eye. 'I'd better not kiss you—I may not be answerable for the consequences.'

'Coward!' she said with a mock pout.

He had never been one to resist a challenge. He kissed her firmly, then just as firmly stepped back. 'Goodnight, my dear.'

'Goodnight,' she said softly. As she went back to her room, with its tumbled bed and the remains of their midnight feast, her heart was singing in her breast. David's desire for her, tempered with tenderness, had been all she could have wished. She was not sure whether she was glad or sorry that Jessica had terminated their lovemaking; had she not, would they have stopped anyway? Or would they have been swept by their mutual desire to a final fulfilment? She would never know ... in one way it did not seem to matter, for David's care and concern for her had appeased her deepest needs....

CHAPTER EIGHT

It was not until the next morning when Anne took breakfast up to Jessica that she realised who had been missing last night—Sonja. 'Where's Miss Sorensen, Jess?' she asked with pretended casualness.

'She went away the day after you did,' Jessica replied, with a certain air of satisfaction. 'She had to go and see somebody. But she's coming back.'

'I see.' It seemed odd that Sonja should have gone away at the same time as Anne. With a cold pang of fear, she wondered if David's enjoyment of her company last night had sprung only from Sonja's absence. Had he made do with second best? It was a depressing train of thought and not one she wished to pursue; she wanted to treasure the memory of those minutes of happiness instead.

David was closeted in his study most of the day, making long-distance calls and working on a brief for a case he was to defend in Charlottetown. So Anne spent most of the day with Jessica. The child was much better, although tired and heavy-eyed after her illness. They read books and coloured pictures, and Anne even sneaked Rover upstairs for a short visit; she had a feeling David would not have approved. She ate all her meals in Jessica's room, and it was only as she carried the supper tray downstairs that she heard Sonja's voice coming from David's study, and knew the blonde had returned.

Deirdre came out of the dining room. 'You didn't need to bring the tray down, dearie, I would have got it.'

'That's all right,' Anne smiled. 'I'll take Jess up a glass of water and settle her for the night.'

David must have heard the sound of their voices. As he came out of the study, Anne's heart flipped in her breast, for she had not seen him since last night. Shyly she said,

'Jessica was wondering if you'd go up and say goodnight to her.'

'Yes, I'll do that.' His voice was clipped to the point of rudeness. Anne looked at him in dismay, for he had become a hard-eyed stranger again; the ease and intimacy of last night was gone. Sonja, she thought bitterly. Sonja's back. I'm only of use when she's not around.

'Once Jessica's asleep,' he went on, 'please will you come down to the study? Sonja wants to see you.'

'Very well,' she replied coolly, her head held high even though inwardly she only wanted to weep for their lost and all too brief companionship. 'Does it concern Jessica?'

'I gather only indirectly,' was the infuriatingly unrevealing response. Turning away, he ran lightly up the stairs, and more slowly Anne followed him. Already she could feel her stomach cramping with nervousness. She had no idea what Sonja could want to discuss, but she sensed it boded her no good.

When, half an hour later, she tapped on the study door, it was Sonja's voice that said, 'Come in.' The tall blonde was reclining in the armchair by the fire; she was as chic and immaculately groomed as always. But under this veneer of sophistication glittered an unmistakable air of triumph. Irresistibly Anne was reminded of one of Jessica's nursery rhymes, 'Step into my parlour, said the spider to the fly'... Sonja had that same aura of gloating cruelty.

'Can I pour you a drink?' David asked.

'I'll have a sherry, thank you,' said Anne, accepting it with a poise that plainly irritated Sonja. 'May I sit down?' she asked with deliberate provocation. 'Or am I supposed to remain standing for this—er—discussion?'

'I think you'd better sit down,' Sonja said spitefully. 'It may take a while.'

Gracefully Anne took the other armchair, very much aware that David had taken up his favourite stance by the fireplace, his blue eyes guarded and watchful.

'Aren't you going to ask me how I enjoyed my little trip?' Sonja said to Anne.

Knowing she was being baited, Anne kept her voice empty of feeling. 'I think you're going to tell me, whether I ask or not. So why don't you go ahead?'

Sonja's red-tipped fingers curled around her glass—like the claws of a predator, Anne thought in a kind of horrified fascination. 'I went to Fredericton first, and then to Halifax.'

She paused suggestively, but all Anne said was, 'Really? How very interesting,' as she took a sip of sherry.

'Yes, interesting is the right word.' Sonja leaned forward, unable to keep the venom out of her face. 'In Fredericton I visited the day-care centre where you used to work, Miss Winters.'

The fight was in the open now. Unobtrusively Anne took a steadying breath. 'Oh? How was Mrs Rippon?' She glanced up at David. 'She was my boss there. You saw the letter from her, I believe.'

'Once I told her I was a friend of Marianne Winters, she was very friendly. She took me around the whole centre—I even saw the room where you used to work.'

Another of those loaded pauses. Anne concentrated on keeping her fingers relaxed in her lap. 'It was a very pleasant room to work in—we always got the afternoon sun.'

'There were photographs hanging on the wall. Photographs of different groups of children with their nurse, whose name was Marianne Winters.' Deliberately Sonja finished her drink and said to David, 'Pour me another one, David, will you, please?'

Too courteous to do otherwise, David went over to the bar. Sensitive as she was to his every mood, Anne knew he was seething with impatience—and with something else, to which she could not put a name. As he placed the glass on the arm of Sonja's chair, she gave him an intimate little smile. 'Thank you, darling. Now, where was I?'

'The photographs, Miss Sorensen,' Anne said levelly, determined that the other woman should not see the sick fear that was pervading her.

'Ah yes, of course.' She ran her eye insolently over

Anne's slender figure. 'You have changed a great deal since those photographs were taken three months ago. The nurse in the photographs, who Mrs Rippon assured me was Miss Marianne Winters, was short and plump with curly brown hair.'

'There must be some mistake,' said Anne. She clasped her hands in her lap, for her fingers were showing a regrettable tendency to tremble.

'That is what I thought,' Sonja said smoothly. 'So I made my farewells to Mrs Rippon and proceeded to Halifax. Although not before Mrs Rippon disclosed that Marianne Winters had left Fredericton to be married, and then to emigrate to Australia. Another mistake, perhaps?'

'I hate to hurry you, when you're so obviously enjoying yourself,' Anne snapped, 'but why don't you get to the point?'

'In Halifax I discovered two things. On January the twenty-fifth, Marianne Winters married Jim Blanchard and the same day they both flew to Australia. And secondly, a Mrs Anne Metcalfe was employed as a nurse at the general hospital for two years; she terminated her employment at the end of January.'

There was no sense in trying to argue. Anne said bitterly, 'You're wasting your talents trying to snag David for a husband, Miss Sorensen. You should be a detective.'

Two red spots flared in Sonja's cheeks at the contempt in Anne's tone. 'So there you have it, David,' she said viciously. 'Your prim and proper Miss Winters is not Miss Winters at all. She is Anne Metcalfe, your ex-wife, and the mother of Jessica.' She turned to Anne. 'Do you deny it?'

'Of course not,' Anne said wearily. 'What would be the use?' She was suddenly so exhausted by the strain of the past half hour that she leaned back in her chair, closing her eyes. All she could see was Jessica's little face. A terrible dread seized her—she would have to leave, now that David knew who she was. He would never allow her to stay. . . .

Sonja said peevishly, 'David, you are saying nothing. Do

you not understand? She is not Marianne Winters—she is your ex-wife.'

'Allow me to make a correction, Sonja. She is not my ex-wife——'

'But she is!'

'If you would let me finish—she is not my ex-wife. She's my wife.'

It was obvious Sonja did not care for his choice of words. 'Is that all you have to say?' she demanded. 'All right, so she's your wife. She needn't be that for long. Now that you know who and where she is, you can divorce her.'

'I see.' His movements so calm and deliberate that Anne thought she would scream, David bent and put another log on the fire.

'You don't seem very upset about the deception she's played on you,' Sonja said sharply. 'I expected more of a reaction from you.'

'Did you now?' he murmured.

Anne willed herself to stop shaking. There were undercurrents here she did not understand, for Sonja was right—David looked very much in control of himself.

'I don't understand how you were so easily deceived,' Sonja persisted. 'You did live with her nearly two years, did you not? Why didn't you recognise her?'

'You're jumping to all the wrong conclusions, Sonja,' he replied evenly. 'She didn't deceive me at all. From the very first time I saw her, I knew exactly who she was.'

The silence was absolute. Before Sonja could speak, Anne got up and went to stand behind her chair, holding on to its back to keep her hands steady. 'How did you know?' she said in a faint voice that was hardly recognisable as her own.

He gave a mocking laugh that made her temper flare. 'My dear wife——'

'Don't call me that!'

'Why not?' he rapped, his eyes as cold as a winter sky. 'It's the truth, isn't it?'

Her fingers tightened their hold, but she could not defy

him for long. 'Yes, it's true,' she said finally, defeated by his iron will. 'But how did you know?'

'As Sonja pointed out not long ago, I did live with you for nearly two years. In conditions of considerable intimacy, I might add.' His eyes roamed her body with an insolence that made her cheeks flame. 'You've matured in the interim —you used to be too thin. But I always did say you had the most beautiful ankles and feet of any woman I've ever seen. I would have known them anywhere.'

Anne flushed with shame, for despite the implied compliment, his voice had been almost totally disinterested. 'So all along you knew who I was?' she said stiffly.

'Precisely.'

Shrilly Sonja interrupted, 'Why did you say nothing?'

'Oh, I thought it would be interesting to see how things developed. And I was rather enjoying it.' His gaze flicked over Anne contemptuously. 'You've become quite an accomplished little actress in the past four years.'

'And you've become more despicable than you ever were! You've been playing with me, amusing yourself at my expense. How could you?'

'Very easily. Besides, I was curious about why you'd come back. I thought I might find out if I waited for a while.'

'Why I came back is my business—but it was certainly not to see you!'

His eyes travelled from the curve of her mouth to her breasts. 'I remember one or two occasions when I thought otherwise.'

Utterly humiliated, she gasped, 'I hate you—oh, God, how I hate you! I hope you do marry Sonja. You deserve each other!' She whirled and ran from the room, knowing she could endure no more. Neither Sonja or David would see her cry, she had that much pride left. So it was not until she was in her own room, with the door tightly closed, that she would allow the tears to spill over and rain down her cheeks. Even so she wept silently, because she could not risk disturbing Jessica. Her shoulders drooping, she saw ahead of her a bleak and empty future in which she was deprived of her daughter's presence by her own husband, whom by one of fate's bitter ironies she still loved.

For the next three days life went on with disconcerting normality. Although Anne had been braced for almost anything after the disastrous session in the study, nothing had happened. She had not been summoned to the study again, or dismissed, or served with divorce papers. Indeed, she had not even seen David at all. Sonja and he were rarely home, and when they were, Anne avoided them assiduously. From the deep subconscious fear that her time with her daughter might be running out, she threw all her care and energy into Jessica.

But the strain of not knowing her fate was beginning to tell on her. She was sleeping poorly, and when she did sleep was haunted by nightmares, visions of nameless horrors that left her tired and weary-eyed. She jumped at the slightest sound. Even her appetite vanished, much to Deirdre O'Connor's concern.

'Now, dearie, you must eat,' she would say, as Anne would pass back her plate almost untouched. 'I do hope you're not catching the 'flu.'

How simple if that were all that was wrong with her! Anne thought wryly. It would almost be a relief to be ill; at least she might rid herself of this gnawing tension, this sense of an axe poised above her head to strike.

On the fourth day David had a visitor: a slight grey-haired man in a pinstripe suit, carrying a briefcase, who arrived in a chauffeur-driven Jaguar. Anne and Jessica were playing outdoors, and he spoke to them pleasantly enough, although Anne sensed the presence of a keen and enquiring mind behind those mild brown eyes. But then she forgot about him for Jessica wanted to take Rover for a walk.

It was Sonja who enlightened her later in the day, when by chance—or at least Anne assumed it was chance—the two women passed each other on the stairs. 'He has come,' Sonja said maliciously.

'Who?'

'The lawyer. You were outside when he came, weren't

you? I imagine he and David are discussing the matter of your divorce right now.'

It was one thing to have contemplated this happening sometime in the future, another to have it brought to the immediate present. Grimly Anne fought back a wave of dizziness. 'Excuse me,' she said with all the composure she could muster, 'Jessica is waiting for me upstairs.'

When she looked out of the upstairs window half an hour later, the Jaguar had gone. She had not even been consulted, she thought bitterly. But then David would see no necessity to do that—to him she was expendable, an object to be removed so he could marry Sonja.

She went to bed early. Perhaps because she now knew her fate, and the days of uncertainty were ended, she fell into a deep sleep, too deep for dreams. And too deep to hear the commotion of people in the hallway, of suitcases being loaded into the car, of Terence driving away. It was Jessica who broke the news the next morning.

'Guess what!' she crowed, bouncing up on Anne's bed.

Anne rubbed her eyes. She felt almost dazed with sleep. She looked at her little alarm clock, scarcely able to believe she had slept so long. 'What?' she mumbled.

'Sonja's gone home!'

Anne blinked, a puzzled frown on her forehead; she entirely forgot to reprimand Jessica for calling the woman by her first name. 'That's impossible!'

'No—I heard Dee-dee telling Terence. "Gone for good and good riddance." What does "good riddance" mean, Anne?'

'Well, it means the person won't be missed. But you must be mistaken, Jess.'

'She went last night. She was in a huff, Dee-dee said, because she didn't get her man.'

Belatedly, Anne applied a little discipline. 'Sweetheart, you mustn't listen to other people's conversations.'

'Why not? It was only about Sonja.'

'Because it's rude—and it's Miss Sorensen to you, not Sonja.'

'What man didn't she get, Anne?'

Anne found herself quite unable to answer this. 'I don't think we should discuss it any further. You go and get dressed, and I'll do the same. I'll race you down to breakfast.'

Needless to say Jessica won, for all of Anne's movements seemed to be in slow motion. They slowed down even more when she saw that David was eating breakfast with Jessica in the alcove; she would have given anything to be able to retreat. Instead, she pulled up her chair and sat down, avoiding David's eyes.

'Good morning, Anne.'

She winced at his use of her real name. 'Good morning.' With sudden bravado she decided to carry the war into the enemy's camp. 'Do I understand from Jessica that Sonja has left?'

'You do.'

'That was rather unexpected, wasn't it?'

'To Sonja, certainly,' was the dry response. 'Not to me. Jessica, pass me the sugar, please, dear. By the way, Jess, do you want to go skiing this morning for a while? It looks as though I'll be in Charlottetown the rest of the day—I might not get back until fairly late.'

'Okay. That'll be fun.'

'Have you finished your breakfast? Then why don't you go and help Terence wax your skis? I think a blue wax would be fine, it's not that cold.'

Jessica ran out eagerly, and David got up to close the door behind her, effectively sealing himself and Anne off from the kitchen. As he sat down again, she eyed him with some misgivings, wishing that his presence did not affect her so greatly. He was wearing a fisherman's knit sweater with dark brown cords, casual clothes in which he looked totally masculine. He also, she thought crossly, looked completely relaxed. It wasn't fair. She was only too aware of the nervous flutter of her pulse as he looked at her across the table.

'I would gather that both you and Sonja have been labouring under a misapprehension this past week.'

She frowned, not understanding his allusion. 'Has she really gone?'

'Oh, yes—and I very much doubt if she'll be back for a while.'

Although Anne could not help being pleased by this, she was still waiting to see if she would be offered any explanation. 'Quite honestly, I can't say I'll miss her. But what was this misapprehension you're talking about?'

'There will be no divorce.'

The colour drained from her face; her relief was so intense that for a moment she thought she would faint. When she was able to speak, she said quietly, 'Sonja told me your visitor yesterday was the lawyer who was looking after the divorce.'

'She was wrong. He was a friend of mine from Toronto, who wouldn't touch a divorce case for love nor money. When I explained to Sonja that a divorce was out of the question, she decided to leave. Just to keep the record straight, at no time have I ever led her to expect any prospects of a marriage between us.'

Anne was silent, for the very good reason that she could think of nothing to say.

'You want a divorce, don't you, Anne?'

He had completely misinterpreted her silence; instead of relief he had picked up disappointment and frustration. Stalling for time, she asked, 'Why do you say that?'

'Why else would you have come back?' His voice was caustic. 'What were you hoping to do—collect the evidence you'd need?'

'No. Although it wouldn't have been very difficult with Sonja around.'

'Just how am I supposed to interpret that?'

'I know you slept together.'

'Oh, do you? How?'

'I—I couldn't sleep one night last week. By accident, I saw you kissing her, and then I heard a bedroom door close —only one door.'

'That, my dear, was Sonja slamming her door in a fit of

pique because I chose not to sleep with her. So much for that piece of evidence.'

Anne stared at him. It could be true ... or it could be a plausible lie, and one that would be impossible to disprove.

'So you can't get a divorce that way, Anne,' David went on. 'I'm sorry to disappoint you. But you should remember that when we first married, I told you I would never accept the idea of a divorce. That hasn't changed, nor will it.'

'Why are you so sure I want one?'

'Because I can't understand otherwise why you should have come back. Did Jonathan put you up to it?'

'No!' she exploded. 'It was nothing to do with him.'

'You can hardly expect me to believe that. What were you hoping for—custody of Jessica?'

'David——'

He disregarded her. 'You'll never get it, so don't try. There's not a judge in the country who would give Jessica to you after the past four years.'

Incensed that he could have so poor an opinion of her motives, Anne exclaimed, 'Will you please listen to me for a minute? What do you think I am, anyway—some kind of a monster? I'd never try and take Jessica from you, that would be a cruel thing to do.'

'It's about what I'd expect from you,' he grated, his mouth a thin line in a face as hard as granite.

'I at least wouldn't deprive her of one of her parents!'

'Just what do you mean by that?'

She laughed mirthlessly, her eyes a blazing green. 'You know perfectly well what I mean.'

There was a tap at the door and Jessica burst in. 'Aren't you ready yet, Daddy?' she exclaimed.

In a lightning-swift change of mood, David smiled at his daughter. 'Sure, let's go.' He glanced at the woman sitting across the table. 'We'll continue this discussion at another more appropriate time.'

None of the retorts that sprang to Anne's mind could be uttered in Jessica's presence—as well David knew. She cast him a smouldering look, saying with blatant untruthfulness, 'I shall look forward to that.'

She spent the morning in the house mending some of Jessica's clothes, an occupation that while it busied her fingers, left her mind free to wander over the confusing events of the past few days. Her mood swung from elation that David wished her to remain his wife, to depression that he—of all people—should be so harsh in his judgments of her. She found herself wishing that he would go away for a few days, just to give her a breathing space, time to accustom herself to the idea that ever since she had arrived, he had known who she was. But when he sought her out right after lunch, while Jessica was having her nap, it was news of a different sort that he had for her.

'I'm giving Terence and Deirdre a couple of days off,' he said abruptly. 'Her sister had to go into hospital unexpectedly, so Deirdre wants to go and look after the family—there are three young children.'

'I hope it's nothing serious?'

'A routine appendectomy. But even that can be a problem with small children that need looking after.'

She must have looked surprised at his understanding and sympathy.

'I'm not a complete ogre,' he snapped. 'I do have a few human qualities.'

'It's a pity I see so little of them.'

'You really are a bitch, aren't you?' he said conversationally. 'However, I didn't come here to discuss your personality, fascinating though it undoubtedly is. While Deirdre is away, I can get a woman from the village to do the housework. Could you look after meals for the three of us?'

'Oh, yes—after all, that's a wife's role, isn't it?'

So suddenly that she jumped, David slammed his clenched fist on the table. 'Lay off—do you hear me?'

'I'm sorry,' she faltered, knowing that she had deliberately provoked his anger. 'I shouldn't have said that.'

His anger vanished as quickly as it had appeared, and for

a moment he looked so tired and discouraged that she longed to comfort him. But then his face hardened to a mask of reserve. 'I won't be home for dinner tonight, so it'll only be the two of you.'

'All right,' she said, wondering with whom he would eat—it was unlikely he would dine in solitude.

'What are your plans for the rest of the day?' he asked.

'I hadn't thought about it,' she said vaguely. 'I expect we'll take Rover for a walk, and maybe go tobogganning. Nothing very ambitious.'

'So you'll just be around the house?'

'I imagine so,' Anne said in faint surprise; he did not normally pay much attention to her daily routine.

He appeared to be satisfied. 'Okay,' he said absently. 'I'd better be off, then. Tell Jessica she and I can go skiing again tomorrow morning if she wants to. Maybe you should go and see Deirdre for a few minutes before she leaves—she'll probably have last-minute instructions for you.'

Not bothering to say goodbye, he left the room. What had she expected, Anne asked herself mockingly—a husbandly kiss? Now that he had gone, she could acknowledge the uneasiness she had been feeling ever since he had told her that Deirdre and Terence would be gone for a few days. What that meant, of course, was that once Jessica was in bed, she and David would be virtually alone in the house, a prospect that alarmed her; tonight she must be sure to be in her own room before he got back.

That was not to be. When Jessica got up, she had a plan for the afternoon all worked out. 'Let's visit the Haleys,' she announced. 'Please, Anne?'

Anne had heard Jessica and Deirdre speak of this family before; they lived a half mile down the road, had three small boys and a host of different animals, so Anne could understand the attraction. 'Should we phone first, do you think?'

'No,' said Jessica with a comical air of wisdom. 'They like people to drop in.'

'Well, all right then.' So shortly afterwards they set off

down the road, both wrapped up warmly in ski suits against the chill Atlantic wind. The Haley's farmhouse was set back from the road, with a long driveway lined by maples. There was a cluster of barns and outbuildings painted white with red trim, and a neatly fenced paddock.

Hoping that Jessica was right about the dropping in, Anne pressed the doorbell. A slight red-haired girl opened the door. 'Hi, Jessica,' she said warmly. 'Come in. The boys are upstairs playing, they'll be glad to see you.' She smiled at Anne, a smile that gave her pointed face a delicate prettiness. 'Hello. I'm Jenny Haley.'

'I'm Marianne Winters.'

'But I call her Anne,' Jessica interposed.

'Then so shall I. Do come in, Anne, and meet the rest of the family. We'd heard of your arrival and hoped you'd come for a visit.'

The rest of the family comprised Jenny's older brother Bill, the owner of the farm, and his wife Marjorie, recuperating from an operation on her spine, together with three boys ranging in age from ten to five. Jessica and the boys disappeared immediately and Jenny settled Anne in a corner of the living-room, where Marjorie was resting on a cot. 'I'll make us all a cup of tea,' Jenny said. 'Anything you need, Marjorie?'

'No, I'm fine.' Marjorie was in her mid-thirties, still pale and thin from her recent ordeal, but with a serenely beautiful face and a warmth of manner that Anne found instantly appealing. 'It's so nice to have visitors, Anne,' she explained. 'I still have to spend a lot of time flat on my back, and the hours get long sometimes. Jenny's been such a marvellous help, but with all the housework to do, she's not getting much time for her painting.'

'Oh? She paints?'

'Yes—and very well, I think, although admittedly I'm prejudiced. She gave up a promising career on the West Coast to come here and look after me. I'm so worried she'll be set back permanently as far as her art is concerned.'

'I wonder if she'd let me see some of her work?'

'I'm sure she would—why don't you go and ask her?'

Rather diffidently Anne made her way to the kitchen. 'Marjorie was telling me you paint,' she said to Jenny. 'May I see some of your paintings?'

'Sure. Right through there.' And Jenny gestured into the light and airy sun-porch that opened off the kitchen.

As Anne went around looking from picture to picture, she grew more and more excited. She had spent enough time with Jonathan visiting various artists and going to different galleries, to know quality when she saw it. And Jenny's work had quality. She painted with an almost photographic reality which by its very attention to detail caused mundane objects to be transcended into an undeniable beauty. Thinking hard, Anne heard Jenny call, 'Tea's ready!'

She walked back into the living-room and said bluntly, 'Jenny, a good friend of mine in Halifax is the director of Maritime Galleries. I'd like to phone him and have him see your paintings; I can't promise anything, but I'm almost sure he'd be interested.'

Jenny's hand remained poised, holding the teapot, while her whole face lit up; the prettiness Anne had discerned earlier became an ethereal beauty. 'Do you really think he'd come?'

'Yes, I think so.'

'It might be just the chance I'm looking for. I'd like to stay on the Island, Anne, but it's been so discouraging trying to get started again.'

'I'll phone him tomorrow.'

Laughing excitedly, Jenny raised her teacup. 'To the future!' she proclaimed. Hurriedly finishing her tea, she added, 'Would you excuse me? I could work on that still life while the light's still good.'

After she had gone, Anne and Marjorie settled down for a chat, and before Anne knew it, Bill, Marjorie's husband, had come in from his barn work. He was a large, fair-haired man of forty or so, who plainly adored his wife. As he bent and kissed her, he said, 'You look better today, love.'

'I've been enjoying Anne's company. Anne, this is my husband, Bill. Bill, Anne Winters, who's looking after Jessica Metcalfe. Oh, Bill, a friend of Anne's runs an art gallery in Halifax. And Anne thinks he'll come over to look at Jenny's paintings. Wouldn't that be wonderful?'

He grinned at Anne wholeheartedly. 'It sure would. I think that calls for a celebration—how about a sherry before dinner? You'll stay and eat with us, Anne?'

'Oh, that would be too much trouble,' she protested.

'He's a great cook,' Marjorie laughed. 'And you'll probably get commandeered to help with the dishes afterwards. Please do stay.'

'I'd love to, then.' She wanted nothing more than to stay, because she could feel herself relaxing and expanding in the friendly atmosphere of the Haleys. Jenny came out of the studio, and Anne was put to work setting the table, keeping up a conversation with Marjorie as she did so. With a minimum of fuss Jenny and Bill produced a delicious meal of deep-fried scallops with hot rolls and a tossed salad, followed by a strawberry shortcake heaped with whipped cream. Anne insisted on washing the dishes, and then they all joined in a riotous game of cards. The time passed quickly; Anne was horrified when she looked at her watch and saw it was after nine. 'Goodness, Jessica,' she exclaimed, 'it's way past your bedtime. We must go.'

'You'll come again, though,' Marjorie said from the cot.

'I will,' Anne promised. 'I've really enjoyed myself, thank you.'

'I'll drive you home,' said Bill.

Even so, it was nearly nine-thirty by the time Bill dropped them off at Stornaway. The house was brightly lit, and Anne could only conclude that David had got home earlier than he had expected. She waved goodbye to Bill and then she and Jessica went round to the back door, Jessica by now dragging her feet. As Anne was taking off Jessica's ski suit she heard her say sleepily, 'Hi, Daddy.'

'Hi, Jess, I was beginning to wonder where you were.'

There was something in the timbre of his voice that made

Anne look up sharply, even though Jessica had not noticed anything amiss and was chattering away to her father. 'We went to the Haleys. The boys showed me the kittens in the barn.' She yawned hugely. 'Carry me upstairs, Daddy?'

'Sure. I'll put you to bed if you like. Anne, I'll see you afterwards.'

It was not a request but an order—and one she had no desire to obey. 'I'm tired too. If you don't mind, I'd really prefer to go straight to bed.'

Over Jessica's head his blue eyes glittered with suppressed anger. 'I do mind,' he said inflexibly. 'I won't keep you long.' He looked down at his daughter, his whole face softening. 'Say goodnight to Anne, pet.'

Anne had no intention of stepping any closer to David in order to kiss Jessica. 'I'll come up and say goodnight in a couple of minutes, Jess,' she said, daring David to contradict her.

When she went upstairs, Jess was already tucked in bed, her eyes drooping. She gave Anne a kiss, then insisted on kissing David again. 'I like having you both here. It's like having a mummy as well as a daddy,' she said drowsily. She could have had no idea of the effect of her words, which Anne felt like a physical blow. She *was* Jessica's mother, but it was a position that David had denied her. Unable to look at him, she left the room and hurried downstairs, knowing all too well that he would follow. He came into the study behind her, his mouth grim.

'Why the hell didn't you tell me this morning that you were planning to go to the Haleys'?'

'Because I didn't know.'

'It just happened,' he said sarcastically.

'Exactly.' Although her heart was beating erratically, she did her best to look composed. 'It was Jessica's idea, actually, and I couldn't see any harm in it.'

'Then why didn't you leave me a note, telling me where you were?'

His inquisition was making her angry. 'One, because you had told me you wouldn't be back until late. Two, because

I hadn't expected to be gone long. But we were invited for supper and so we stayed.' Only wanting to hurt him, she flailed out, 'It was good for both of us to see how a *real* family lives.'

'Don't push me too far—I'm not in the mood for your bitchy remarks. Look at it from my point of view for a minute. I got back at eight-thirty, the house was in darkness, there was no sign of you or Jessica and I had no idea where you were. What the devil was I supposed to think?'

'I don't know,' she said slowly, hit by a sudden insight. 'But I know what you did think. You thought I'd left and taken Jessica with me, didn't you?' She laughed wildly. 'Stolen her ... kidnapped her ... that's what you thought!'

He did not bother to deny it. 'Do you blame me?'

Anne felt like crying, that he could consider her capable of such a dreadful deed. 'Oh, I know there's no limit to the things you think I'll do. But for once you might try trusting me—I did tell you I would never come between you and Jessica, and I meant it.'

'Trust you! My dear Anne, after what happened four years ago, I'll never trust you again.' Although she tried to speak, David ignored her and went on harshly, 'I just wish I knew why you came back. No doubt your twisted little motives will surface sooner or later——'

'Why do you hate me so?' she whispered, her grey eyes bleak with pain.

'Spare me that routine,' he sneered. 'And for God's sake don't start to cry. It's the oldest trick in the book.'

'I have no intention of crying. You're not worth it!'

'You're a fine one to talk that way!'

'Instead of standing here trading insults with you. I'm going to bed,' she said, hoping he had missed the tremor in her voice; she did not know how much more of this she could stand.

'Then allow me to exercise my husbandly prerogative and kiss you goodnight before you go.'

Anne backed away, her eyes enormous. 'That won't be necessary.'

'Just be glad it's only a kiss I'm asking for, Anne. Don't forget I *am* still your husband—I could be demanding a great deal more than a kiss.'

'You wouldn't,' she stammered.

'Don't count on it.'

In three long strides he was between her and the door. She was frozen to the spot by the ice-cold brilliance of his eyes. In spite of herself, she started to shiver.

'Come here, Anne.'

Like a rabbit paralysed by a snake, she stood rooted to the spot. 'Please, no——'

'Then I'll have to come to you.'

Closer and closer, until she could see the pulse hammering at the base of his throat ... almost sick with fear, she suffered the steel strength of his embrace, the hard pressure of his lips on hers. She was shaking so hard she could hardly stand.

Then he thrust her away, his mouth an ugly line, his fists clenched at his sides. 'Rape never was my speciality,' he snarled. 'Go to bed, for God's sake!'

Before he could change his mind, she turned and fled from his presence, seeking the sanctuary of her own room. It only she could lock the door ... she sank down on the bed, drawing in her breath in long, quivering sighs until eventually she felt calmer. Now that she was alone, her desperate fear seemed an overreaction; but she had only to remember the pent-up hatred and frustration in David's eyes to feel a claustrophobic panic close around her again.

She lay awake for a long time, terrified of hearing footsteps approach her door, and a man's hand open it.

CHAPTER NINE

SHE did not awaken until the sunlight was streaming across her bed; presumably Jessica had overslept too, after her late night. In the sober light of day, Anne's fear seemed groundless. David had only been trying to frighten her, and it was unfortunate she had allowed him to succeed so admirably. She was sure now he had not been serious in his threat to exercise his rights over her body, but because she had been tired and overwrought, she had exaggerated a fairly simple situation into one of nightmare proportions. She must not allow it to happen again, although there was no denying she would feel safer when Deirdre and Terence returned.

It was not until after lunch that Anne remembered her promise to get in touch with Jonathan about Jenny's paintings—now would be a good time, while Jessica was having her afternoon rest. She was almost sure David was working in the study, so she decided to use the extension in the kitchen, and got through to the gallery without any difficulty. 'May I speak to Mr Maxwell, please?'

'Certainly. Who's calling, please?'

'Anne Metcalfe.'

In a couple of minutes Jonathan came on the line. 'Anne! How are you? What a nice surprise!'

'Why, thank you,' she laughed, immeasurably cheered by his pleasure.

'How are things going?'

'Well, pretty awful, actually,' she confessed. 'Apart from Jessica, of course. But that's not why I called, Jon. Yesterday I visited some people down the road, and there's a young girl staying there, a Jenny Haley, who's a painter. I saw about twenty of her works. Jonathan, they're good. I'd really like you to come and see them. Will you?'

Even over the telephone she could sense his caution.

'Are you sure, Anne? What medium does she use? Any particular style?'

The discussion became fairly technical, but in the end Anne's enthusiasm must have convinced him. 'Well, I'll have a look at them,' he said. 'As a matter of fact, I have tomorrow afternoon free; an appointment I'd had has just been cancelled. I'll get a flight over and hire a car at the airport—I'll phone you when the plane gets in, how's that?'

'That's lovely, Jonathan, thank you. I'm sure you won't be disappointed.'

He chuckled. 'You've visited enough artists with me that you should know what you're talking about!'

'Such conceit!' she teased. 'I'll see you tomorrow.'

'Okay, hon. Goodbye.'

She put down the phone, a smile lingering on her face. She'd known she could depend on him ... dear Jonathan. And wouldn't it be nice if he was as impressed with Jenny Haley herself, as with her paintings? He deserved far more than she, Anne, could give him. ...

'Who were you talking to?' David's voice demanded.

Her head snapped around. 'To Jonathan.'

'Where is he?'

'In Halifax. If you're worried about the phone call being long distance, you can deduct it from my salary.'

He ignored this red herring. 'Just how are you going to see him tomorrow?'

'You were listening!'

'Unintentionally, I assure you. But you haven't answered my question.'

'He's coming over here tomorrow afternoon.'

'So you can cry on his shoulder and tell him how badly I treat you?'

'No, it's nothing like that——'

'Anne, let's get something straight once and for all. You're my wife, and you'll remain my wife. You'd better make that clear to your friend Jonathan. And then maybe he'll stop dangling after you.'

She was damned if she'd tell him the truth about Jonathan's visit now. If he wanted to think the worst of her, let him. There was nothing new about that, after all.

'I came down to tell you that Jessica's awake. I still have some work to do, so maybe you could amuse her for a while.'

She couldn't help herself. 'Are you sure you trust me with her?'

He ran his fingers through his thick hair, and for a moment his face was tired and defenceless. 'Yes, Anne. If there's one thing I know, it's that you're good for Jessica. If you hadn't been, you would have been gone long ago, wife or no wife. Oh, yes—you love Jessica.' There was the slightest of emphasis on the last word.

Puzzled, yet strangely heartened, she raised something that had been bothering her. 'David, *you* know I'm your wife, but no one else does. What about Jessica—are we going to tell her?'

His shoulders slumped wearily. 'No—not yet, anyway. If only I could understand——' He broke off. 'Oh, what the hell's the use?'

'David——'

He ignored her unspoken plea. 'I'll be in the study if you need anything.' He turned on his heel and was gone.

Anne gave a sigh of frustration. She had sensed they had been on the verge of real communication, with a possibility of destroying some of the ugly barriers between them. But then he had left—oh, damn!

She didn't see David again until later in the afternoon. She and Jessica, after a strenuous couple of hours constructing a new snow fort, had repaired to the kitchen, and were perched on stools having a mug of cocoa each while they decided on a dinner menu. Anne was wearing slim-fitting cranberry red slacks with a grey and red Fair Isle sweater; her hair waved softly around her face and she was flushed and bright-eyed from the exercise outdoors. Jessica was also rosy-cheeked, so that when David walked in, the two faces that turned towards him were heartbreakingly alike. He stood still for a minute and again Anne saw that bleakness shadow his features.

'Daddy, will you come and see our new fort tomorrow?'

He roused himself with an effort. 'Sure, Jess—is it a big one?'

'Absolutely huge! Can we have hot dogs and french fries for supper?'

David winced. 'How about a nice steak instead, with baked potatoes and a salad? And Deirdre left some cream puffs in the freezer.'

'She didn't tell me about those,' Anne teased.

He laughed, his blue eyes for once meeting hers without any hidden messages. 'They were my secret.'

'Glutton!'

'I'm offering to share them, aren't I?' he said in mock hurt.

And suddenly they were all three laughing together. 'You looked silly like that, Daddy,' Jessica giggled.

'And you lack a proper respect for the older generation, young lady,' her father said severely.

'What does that mean?' Jess asked blankly.

He tousled her hair playfully. 'It means I love you.'

'And I love you!' She nuzzled him unselfconsciously. 'I love Anne, too.'

David's big body grew still. 'Do you?'

'Oh, yes. I wish she could stay for ever and ever.'

His eyes fixed on Anne with a painful intensity. 'Well, you never know, maybe she will.'

Jessica's brow creased thoughtfully. 'If you married her, she'd have to. Wouldn't she?'

'Yes. If I was married to her, she'd have to stay.' David gave himself a shake as his voice came back to normal. 'But that's grown-up's business, pet. Will you scrub the potatoes for me? And maybe Anne would make the salad.'

He looked at Anne so seriously that she felt he was asking for more than the simple question would imply. It was as though he was pleading with her for Jessica's sake to stay 'for ever and ever'—or was she being overly fanciful? Her face equally serious, she said, 'Yes, of course I will.'

His smile broke through, giving his face a vitality and charm that had the power to take her breath away. 'Being a man, I'll look after the important matter of the steak.'

'Chauvinist!' Anne retorted. She walked around him to get to the refrigerator, but as she did so his arm came around her waist, stopping her progress. Feeling her heartbeat quicken, she looked up at him questioningly.

He dropped a kiss on the tip of her nose. 'Thanks,' he said softly.

He was so close she felt herself drowning in the blue depths of his eyes. For what was he thanking her? For the cessation of the hostility and anger that so often kept them apart? For their shared laughter, the brief sense of being a family? 'It was a pleasure,' she said with absolute sincerity.

Simultaneously they became aware that Jessica was observing them with wide-eyed interest. Anne blushed and David said abruptly, 'I'll get you the potatoes, Jess. Roll up your sleeves, okay?'

The next couple of hours would long remain in Anne's memory. By unspoken consent she and David had—at least temporarily—buried the hatchet. As they prepared the meal, they joked and laughed together, and because she was happy, her fragile beauty was illuminated. She could not help noticing how often David brushed against her, or how frequently his hand would rest on her shoulder—she was sure it was not by accident. Because each touch filled her with a poignant delight, her body glowed with awareness of him. As he poured her a glass of wine, his fingers closed over hers, their warmth burning into her flesh. She looked up to find smouldering in his eyes a blatant sexual message of desire. Heat enveloped her body; her lashes trembled over her eyes, in which all her own passionate need of him was openly displayed.

'The steak's burning, Daddy!'

Hurriedly Anne moved away from him. It was a good

thing Jessica was too young to understand the significance
of that silent exchange. She sipped her wine, feeling its
warmth course down her throat, and began to set the table
in the alcove, obeying an inner voice of caution that warned
her to attend to practical matters. David carried in the bowl
of salad and for a moment they were alone. Anne had just
lit the candles on the table, and their light flickered over
her face, accenting her high cheekbones and the mysterious
smoky-grey of her irises.

The caress in his eyes was as palpable as a touch. 'I
want you. God, how I want you!' he said huskily, letting
his gaze drop deliberately to the swell of her breasts and
the rounded curve of her hips. It was as though he had
stripped her naked. A delicious lassitude invaded her limbs
as her lips parted in unconscious invitation. Quietly he
added, 'And you want me just as much as I want you.'

It was useless to deny it. She said weakly, 'We'd better
go back to the kitchen. Jessica will be wondering about us.'

'I love our daughter dearly,' said David in such a low
voice that she had to strain to catch the words, 'but at the
moment I wish she was a thousand miles away.'

That tiny word 'our' caught at her heart, and blindly she
turned away, fleeing to the prosaic surroundings of the
kitchen. She was almost glad Jessica *was* there, for part of
her was frightened by the glowing desire that could so
easily leap into flame between her and David. She forced
herself to remember his cruelty and contempt towards her,
although both now seemed remote and unreal.

The meal was delicious. Afterwards they cleaned up the
kitchen and took coffee and liqueurs to the study; David
lit the fire and Jessica settled down on the rug with her
colouring book. Content to watch the dancing flames, Anne
and David made desultory conversation until finally David
said, 'Bedtime, Jess.'

The child looked from one to the other of the couple on
the chesterfield. 'Will you both read me a story tonight?'
she asked hopefully.

'You're an opportunist!' David chuckled.

Jessica looked understandably puzzled. 'Are you one of those too, Daddy?'

David looked straight at Anne. 'I could be, given the chance.'

Refusing to be sidetracked, Jessica said, 'So will you both read a story?'

'I guess so,' David acquiesced, kneeling down on the rug. 'Hop up, and I'll give you a piggyback.'

As Jessica squealed with delight, burying her fingers in David's thick hair, Anne felt the all-too-familar lump in her throat. Jessica looked so tiny against the broad expanse of David's back; his hands on her body were exquisitely gentle. If it meant never seeing Jessica again, Anne knew she could not come between father and daughter.

Once Jessica was settled down for the night, with Pooh Bear tucked against her cheek, David said to Anne, 'Let's go down and finish our liqueurs.' As they descended the stairs together, all of a sudden Anne could think of nothing to say. The easy friendliness of the past couple of hours had vanished and in its place was a sense of stress and awkwardness. As he held open the study door for her to precede him, she deliberately kept a space between them.

After putting a couple of logs on the fire, he took up his usual stance by the fireplace, staring down into the flames in a withdrawal that was greater than the physical distance between them. Anne curled up on the chesterfield, her feet tucked under her. She wished he would put on some music, if only to cover the silence that lay between them, impenetrable as a wall. She was very much aware that, apart from Jessica, they were alone in the house.

Finally he looked up. She was shocked by the tension in his face; the hand that lay along the mantel was white-knuckled with strain. As he began to speak, she knew he was choosing his words with care. 'Anne, I have to know why you came back—why, after four years of silence, you suddenly appeared again.'

The atmosphere had changed in the room, subtly he had become an antagonist. He continued slowly, 'I've thought of several possible reasons. I need to know the truth, Anne —I need to understand.'

Her attention was riveted on him, her hands tightly clasped in her lap. She heard every cadence of his voice, saw every slight shift of his body, as he went on, 'I thought at first it might be money.' She must have made some move of protest, for he said quickly, 'Don't get upset. It's hard for a woman on her own. I gather from what Sonja said you must have finished your nurse's training and got a job. But I don't imagine your salary was very high and you may have felt I owed you something—you were, after all, my wife. I certainly wouldn't condemn you for that. Did you need money? Did you hope I'd make you an allowance?'

'No! Money had nothing to do with it. I suppose I didn't have much by your standards, but I was independent and self-supporting, and that was enough.'

'I see.' He tried a new tack. 'I've already asked you if you came back to get a divorce.'

'And I've already denied it.'

'Even with Jonathan coming tomorrow? You can't tell me he's not in love with you.'

Anne lowered her eyes. 'Yes, he's in love with me.'

'Has he asked you to marry him?'

Trying not to flinch, she met the unmasked hostility in his expression. 'Yes.'

'Which presupposes a divorce.'

'He asked me to marry him,' she replied, feeling her temper rise in spite of herself. 'But that doesn't mean I said yes.'

David gave a short laugh. 'I suppose not. Well, let's assume you didn't want a divorce—even though I'm not entirely convinced.'

'I've said I didn't! Why don't you try believing me for a change?'

'That brings us to the crux of the matter, doesn't it?' he said hoarsely. 'All right, Anne, let's have your version of why you came to Stornaway.'

She had a strange sensation that she was fighting for her life, and sent up a silent prayer for the wisdom to make him understand. If only they could clear away all the bitter anger that had festered now for four long years! She said quietly and with absolute truth, 'I came to see Jessica.'

'Your maternal feelings do you credit—but they're a little belated, aren't they?'

'That's hardly my fault.'

'I would have thought that was very much your fault.' He leaned forward accusingly. 'Jessica is four years old. Why did it take that long for you to suddenly decide you had to see her? And this whole Marianne Winters business—what the hell was that for?'

She answered his last question first. 'I was scared you might not let me see Jessica if I just came back as myself, so I tried to deceive you.' Her mouth twisted ruefully. 'By the sound of things, I might just as well have saved myself the trouble.'

'You were right to be worried. Anne Metcalfe wouldn't have got in as easily as Marianne Winters. But you still haven't told me why it took you four years to start behaving like a normal mother who wanted to see her child.'

'This is a farce, David!' she exclaimed furiously. 'You know perfectly well why I dropped out of sight——'

'Oh, no, I don't. Any woman who'd walk out on her own baby when it's scarcely a week old—not to mention walking out on her husband—deserves to be horsewhipped.'

'I didn't walk out on my child!'

'Didn't you wait until the nurses' backs were turned, and then calmly leave the hospital? And then didn't you disappear without a trace?'

'Yes, I did, but——'

'God! How could you have done that? I know we weren't getting along very well, Anne, but with a new daughter to share, we could have made our marriage work. I still loved you then.'

His last sentence stabbed her with agony. 'We certainly weren't getting along very well. Remember how you cast doubts on Jessica's paternity? I was never unfaithful to you, never—then.'

He drew in his breath sharply and she knew she had

struck home. Slowly he said, 'I really never believed you had been—I guess it was all part of the crazy life we were leading. Too much excitement, too many parties, too many people.' He walked over to the couch and pulled her to her feet. 'I'm sorry about that, Anne.'

She detached his hands and moved back, her face paper-white. He was apologising for all the wrong things. 'If that were all, I could forgive you easily.'

'What else did I do?' David's eyes narrowed.

At the end of her tether she cried, 'Stop this, David! You know damn well what you did—and it was the cruellest thing in the world! I'll never forgive you for it! Because of you, I've lost the first four years of Jessica's life—lost them for ever. No one can give them back to me.' Tears were streaming down her cheeks and angrily she wiped them away.

David went very still. 'I'm as much in the dark now as I was four years ago,' he said heavily. 'What did I do that was so dreadful, Anne?'

'You lied to me!' she sobbed raggedly. 'You told me you never wanted to see me again and——'

'You've got that the wrong way around. It was *you* who said you didn't want me to come near you.'

But nothing could stop her now. Her voice raw with pain, she whispered, 'And then you told me the baby had died.' She sank back on the couch, covering her eyes with her hands, her shoulders heaving.

With ruthless strength he pulled her hands away. 'I did no such thing!'

It was as though he had not spoken and she flung the words at him. 'I'll always hate you for that!'

'If I had done such a despicable thing, I could hardly blame you for hating me. But I didn't do it, Anne.'

'You did!'

'How could I have?' he retorted, his words frayed with anger. 'I didn't even see you once you went into the hospital.'

Anne looked at him through a blur of tears. Because the message about the baby's death had come from David, she

had sometimes almost forgotten in the intervening years
that it had been Claire, his mother, who had actually delivered the blow.

'No, that's right,' she said bitterly. 'You didn't even have
the courage to do your own dirty work. You sent Claire
instead.'

There was a grim note in his voice. 'One minute I'm the
one who told you Jessica was dead, the next minute it's
Claire. What am I supposed to believe?'

'Oh, you'll believe what you choose to believe,' she said
wearily. 'That was always the way with you.'

'It would help if you got your story straight.'

Electrified by a fury so intense she could hardly speak,
she stormed, 'Story? It was no story—it happened. Why
do you bother denying it, David? Don't tell me that after
all these years you feel ashamed of yourself?'

Speaking with ice-cold clarity, he said, 'I did not at any
time tell you Jessica was dead. Nor did I get Claire to tell
you that.'

'I don't believe you!'

'Stalemate,' he said viciously. He paused for a minute,
fighting for control. 'Anne, for God's sake, listen to me.
You were very young when Jessica was born. I was away,
and there was no one to support you through the ordeal
of childbirth and your illness. I can understand if you felt
frightened of the responsibility of a baby, or if you didn't
want to be tied down. After all, you were only twenty. I
expect it was all too much for you. And if you decided to
walk away from it all, I could hardly blame you. You must
still have been ill when you left the hospital. I don't know
why you didn't get in touch with me, at least to find out
how the baby was, if nothing else, but——'

'You haven't believed a word I've said, have you?' she
said with the calmness of utter despair. She stood up, feeling bruised and battered all over. 'There's no point in con-
tinuing this—I've had all I can take. I'm going to bed.'

He made no move to stop her. 'Running away again?'
he taunted.

'If that's what you want to think. Goodnight.'

Anne more or less fell into bed, too tired to think and certainly with no desire to relive the scene in the study. Almost immediately sleep claimed her and soon she was breathing deeply and regularly.

She was dreaming ... a hand was stroking her, sliding from her shoulders down the indentation of her spine to the curve of her hips. Slowly it continued its sensuous exploration, and she lay warm and relaxed as gently probing fingers found the fullness of one breast, tracing its soft pyramid to the tip, teasing the nipple to hardness. She thought her body would melt with sweetness. Deep within her desire stirred into life and to an aching need for that caressing hand ... she murmured something, half rolling over, and her leg fell against a man's muscular thigh.

Shocked from sleep, she gave a tiny cry of fear, cringing away from the dark shape in her bed.

'Don't be frightened. It's I—David.'

Still not fully awake, her mind fumbled to make sense of what was happening. 'What are you doing here?' she stammered, even as she spoke realising the utter insanity of the question.

Amused, he replied, 'I would have thought that was obvious.'

So she had not been dreaming—the touch she had so warmly responded to had been David's. Shame flushed her cheeks, and she was glad of the concealing darkness. She pulled away, her body rigid with revulsion. 'Go away!' she whispered fiercely, knowing all too well Jessica was sleeping only a few feet away on the other side of the wall.

'I have every right to be here.'

'David, please——' She forgot her pride long enough to beg. 'Please leave my room. I don't want——'

'Yes, you do.'

Anne bit her lip. Cudgelling her brain for some way to get rid of him, she said finally, 'You were asking me this evening why I came back. Whatever the reason, it wasn't for this. You know as well as I do that our marriage is a mockery. I'm your wife in the legal sense, but that's all. And that's the way it's got to be.'

'Why?'

'Because we don't love each other, for a start.' Her eyes were adjusted to the dark now, and she could see that David was lying facing her, his head propped on his elbow. His chest was bare, his hips swathed in the blankets. Trying to keep her voice steady, Anne went on, 'You don't love me— you must despise me to think me capable of walking out on Jessica and staying away for four years. And yet you want to make love to me?' She gave a bitter little laugh. 'Now you're the one who's despicable!'

'If the phrase "to make love" offends you, why don't we just say I lust after you? You have a beautiful body, and I'm only human.'

'There has to be more to sex than just animal appetites,' she argued frantically. 'Oh, David, please go away! I promise I'll stay and look after Jessica for as long as you want me to, and I promise I won't ask you for a divorce— isn't that enough?'

'No.' The monosyllable hung in the air between them.

Anne had not drawn the curtains, and a silver swath of moonlight cast a cold eerie light over the bed. David's eyes seemed to be sunk into sockets in his skull; his mouth was a ruthless gash. She tensed her muscles under the blanket, preparing to leap from the bed and run to Jessica's room. She'd be safe there . . . but before she could move, his hand shot out and grabbed her wrist. Foolishly she was reminded of the steel jaws of the trap that had caught Rover. 'You're hurting,' she faltered, feeling herself being pulled inexorably closer to him. She tried to twist free, kicking out at him under the covers, but all she accomplished was to bare her thighs to the moonlight, her skin alabaster pale against the dark bedspread.

She heard his rapid intake of breath, as he muttered, 'God! You're beautiful. Come here. . . .' Then his other arm came hard around her shoulders. Her breasts were crushed against his chest as the weight of his thighs held her flailing limbs captive.

'No, David——'

His lips, warm and sure, silenced her plea. His hand began to stroke her again. She fought against his hold, writhing like a wildcat, but her struggles only excited him more. He fell across her and flames leaped through her body as she realised just how aroused he was. With dramatic suddenness she knew she no longer wanted to escape. Her lips moved under his in sensuous surrender, and as she felt his hands push her nightdress to her waist she offered no resistance, rejoicing in the silkness of her skin against the rough tangle of hair on his chest. His lips parted hers. His hands sought all the secret places of her body, tormenting her to a crescendo of passion. Fiercely she arched herself against him, her fingernails running down the length of his spine. With all the generosity of her nature, she wanted to give him as much pleasure as he was granting her. She was lost, caught in a whirlpool of desire that sucked her into its vortex. From a long way away, she heard his voice cry out. . . .

Afterwards they lay quietly together, his tawny hair resting on her breast, listening to the slowing of her heartbeat. There was no need for words. Assuaged of hungers she had tried to deny for four long years, satiated by David's tempestuous lovemaking, Anne felt herself drifting on a peaceful sea; lapped by wave after wave of contentment, she let her eyes close. Her dark hair was fanned on the pillow, her hand lay palm up, fingers loosely curled.

It was early dawn when she awoke. The moonlight had been dispelled by the pale light of morning. She knew as she surfaced slowly from a sleep that had been fathoms deep, that something was different . . . something had happened. Her hand moved questingly across the bed, but she was alone. Had it all been a dream? Had she conjured David's presence from the wraiths of sleep and from the strength of her own love and longing?

Bewildered, she turned over. The blankets were tangled and twisted. In the pillow beside hers there was the indentation of a head. And her nightdress lay in a heap on the floor beside the bed.

Huddling under the covers, she buried her face in the

pillow. It was no dream. It had been all too real—David had
shared her bed. As she remembered how shamelessly she
had responded to him, her cheeks burned. Although he
had touched her with a lover's intimacy, he had spoken not
a single word of love, she thought painfully. He had taken
what he wanted, then he had gone, leaving her alone. The
intimacy they had shared had been a false intimacy, and its
very falsity had left her lonelier than she had been for
months. She discovered she was silently weeping, the tears
coursing down her face to soak into the pillow. With a sigh
of defeat, she closed her eyes. How clever of David to keep
asking her why she had come back! She would do well to
ask herself the same question, for just as Jonathan had pre-
dicted, her return to her husband was bringing her nothing
but pain and heartbreak.

CHAPTER TEN

When she went downstairs, it took all her courage to walk into the kitchen where David and Jessica were preparing breakfast. 'Hi, Jessica,' she said with her normal warmth. Her voice trailing away, she added, 'Er—good morning, David.'

His eyes slid over her mockingly. For reasons she had not analysed, she had put on her oldest slacks and a loose-fitting top, and had pulled her hair back ruthlessly into a tight little bun. But as his eyes lingered on her face, she knew he was recalling the very different Anne whose naked body had lain with his. Two spots of colour burning her cheeks, she said brightly, 'What's for breakfast?'

'Bacon'n'eggs,' said Jessica, running the words together. 'You've got purple under your eyes again.'

'Oh,' said Anne blankly, wishing Jessica was not quite as discerning. 'I haven't had my good morning kiss yet.'

'That can be easily remedied,' David's deep voice said. 'Here, hold this, Jess,' and he passed his daughter the spatula before walking over to Anne.

'I meant——'

His mouth cut off whatever else she had been going to say. He kissed her thoroughly, and because she knew Jessica was watching, Anne was helpless to struggle. Adding to her confusion she could feel his hands fumbling at the back of her neck, pulling out the hairpins. When he finally released her, her hair tumbled free to her shoulders.

'That's better,' he said calmly. 'I don't like your hair like that—do you, Jess?'

'It looks nicer now,' the child said judiciously. 'I think the bacon's done, Daddy.'

Thoroughly flustered, Anne watched the two fair heads bend over the frying pan. She might as well set the table,

160

she thought with a touch of wry humour, because she'd obviously had all the attention she was going to get. As she walked back and forth to the alcove, where the sun was streaming through the windows to lie in warm patches on the carpet, she recognised with a sense of fatality that no matter what happened, this was where she wanted to be— here, with Jessica—and with David. She loved him so deeply and irrevocably that it was better to be with him under almost any circumstances than to be separate from him. . . .

'Is this how you want your egg done, Anne?' Jessica called from the kitchen.

Anne gave herself a mental shake and walked over to the stove. 'Perfect!' she exclaimed.

Unselfconsciously Jessica rubbed her curly head against Anne's sleeve. 'This is fun, isn't it?'

Anne knew exactly what she meant. She hugged Jessica, delighting in the child's fragile limbs and silken smooth skin; she was suddenly overwhelmed by a primitive surge of love for this child of hers, a wave of feeling so strong that she had to fight back tears. Jessica noticed nothing unusual. But as Anne looked up she realised David was staring at her, a frown on his brows. His eyes were baffled, an unanswered question in their depths. Then he turned away, severing that puzzling moment of communication.

As they were finishing their meal he said abruptly, 'When is Jonathan arriving?'

'Mid-afternoon, I would think. He said he'd call me from the airport.'

'As you'll be otherwise occupied, then, I'll take the afternoon to go to the university library. I need to do a bit of research for this latest case I'm working on. Jessica can stay with you?'

Did he think she'd be annoyed to have her supposed tête-à-tête with Jonathan spoiled by the addition of Jessica? With a sparkle of mischief in her face, she said demurely, 'Of course. Jonathan is very fond of children.'

'We'll have to hope he can find himself a wife then, won't

we?' David grated, pushing back his chair. 'Jess, do you want to go skiing after a while?'

The day proceeded normally, except that after lunch David took the Mercedes to Charlottetown. Then Jonathan arrived about three-thirty in a rented car. He planted a kiss on Anne's cheek with a matter-of-factness that reassured her. 'Nice to see you.'

She hugged him. 'You too,' she said ungrammatically. 'Let me just write a note to David telling him where we'll be, and then we can go.' Within a few minutes the three of them set off, Jessica perched on Anne's knee. When they arrived, the Haley boys were tobogganing on the hill and beckoned Jessica to join them. As Anne watched her running towards the slope, there was a soft light in her eyes.

'You look more ... content, somehow,' Jonathan remarked.

She turned to face him. 'Yes, I guess I am. This is where I belong, Jonathan.'

'For better, for worse,' he quipped. Although there had been a slight trace of bitterness in his tone, she sensed he was learning to accept her ultimatum.

'Let's go in,' she suggested. 'I do hope you like the paintings, Jonathan.' Now that he was actually here, she was beginning to doubt her judgment, and for the first time realised how terribly awkward it would be for her and for the Haleys if he did not feel the paintings were up to the standards of the gallery.

As before, it was Jenny who opened the door, her big eyes grave in her piquant face. She ushered them both in, introduced Jonathan to Marjorie, and for a few minutes they all exchanged pleasantries. Then Jonathan said in a businesslike manner, 'May I see your paintings, Miss Haley? And perhaps you can tell me something about your training. Have you had any other showings?' The two of them disappeared into Jenny's work area, Jonathan closing the door behind them.

'I'm as nervous as if they were my own paintings,' Marjorie confided.

'So am I,' Anne laughed. 'Let's make a cup of tea while we're waiting—it'll help to pass the time.'

It was well over an hour before Jonathan and Jenny emerged; they were talking together very seriously, and for a moment Anne's heart failed her—he hadn't liked them. But then Jenny caught sight of the two anxious faces and her rare smile lit her face, giving it an elfin charm to which, Anne noticed, Jonathan was by no means blind. 'There'll be an exhibition of the works of Miss Jennifer Haley at the Maritime Galleries, Halifax, Nova Scotia. Opening date March the fifteenth,' she declaimed. 'Oh, Marjorie, Jonathan really likes them! Isn't it exciting?'

So it's 'Jonathan' already, thought Anne with great satisfaction, noticing the pair exchange a quick smile of mutual congratulations before Jenny was gathered into Marjorie's embrace. Bill had just come in from his chores and added his voice to the chorus. Anne waited long enough to make sure Jonathan was to be invited for dinner, then said placidly, 'Would you mind driving me and Jessica home, Bill? I promised David we'd be back for supper.'

'You're sure you can't stay?'

'No, I really must go. Enjoy your dinner, Jonathan. Bill's a mean cook! And I'm so happy for you, Jenny. Marjorie, I'll see you in a day or two.'

At Stornaway the Mercedes was already parked outside the house. Anne sent Jessica upstairs to change her wet clothes, then located David in the study.

His face inscrutable, he said the obvious. 'You're back.'

Still exhilarated by the afternoon's success, she said airily, 'Why, yes—weren't you expecting me?'

'I'm not sure.'

'Didn't you see my note?'

'Yes.' He walked over to the sideboard and poured them both a sherry. 'Where's Jonathan?' he asked, an edge on his voice.

'Oh, he stayed at the Haleys' for dinner.'

'You can't tell me he came all the way from Halifax to see you, and you've left him at the Haleys'?'

Her excitement bubbled over. 'Jenny Haley, Bill's sister, has been looking after Marjorie for the past few weeks. She's an artist. I took Jonathan over there to see Jenny's paintings. I'd been really impressed with them and I was hoping he would be too. And he was! She'll be having a showing in a couple of months, at his gallery.'

'Jenny Haley,' David mused, looking as though he was doing some very rapid mental adjustments, 'I met her once, I believe. Rather an attractive little thing.'

'A very attractive little thing, if you ask me,' Anne said smugly.

'What kind of a game are you playing?' he demanded. 'Aren't you scared Jonathan might fall for her?'

'I'm scared he won't!' she said frankly.

David put down his glass so sharply that the crystal rang. 'Anne, you told me Jonathan was in love with you——'

'That's true. But you never asked if I was in love with him.'

'Well, are you?'

'No. I never have been. He's a dear friend, and he'll always be that. And yes,' she added recklessly, 'I do hope he falls for Jenny Haley. She's a lovely girl and just what he needs.'

'After all these years you can still surprise me,' he said slowly. In what seemed a complete change of subject he asked, 'Where's Jessica?'

'I sent her upstairs to get changed. I expect she's watching television. Cartoons are on.'

'Then this seems like an opportune time to tell you what I've done,' he said quietly, giving her no warning of what was to come. 'I telephoned Claire this afternoon and told her you'd come back. She'll be arriving here in three days.'

Thunderstruck, Anne stared at him, unable to believe the evidence of her own ears. 'Say that again.'

'Claire will be coming here on Saturday,' he repeated patiently.

The colour drained from her face. Her mind flew back

to the hospital room where Clair, so cool and composed, had delivered the words that had shattered her life. 'I don't want to see her!'

'I'm afraid you have no choice. She'll be staying here at the house.'

'For how long? Maybe I could go to Halifax for a couple of days, just while she's here.'

'No, Anne. You'll stay here, where you belong.'

'She hates me,' Anne whispered. 'She always did.' She looked down at her shaking hands. 'I—I'm scared of her, David. Scared of what she'll do. I'm sorry, I know I'm not making much sense, and I know she's your mother, but I'm frightened.'

'You'll find her changed, I think, since you saw her last.'

Nothing could change Claire, Anne though grimly. Cold, determined Claire, who ruled her own life as well as everyone else's with a rod of iron, who had never shown herself capable of any of the gentler emotions ... Claire would not have changed. 'I don't want to see her!' she burst out, her face pinched and hostile. 'Why are you doing this to me?'

'I have reasons—good reasons. But they'll keep until she comes.' He patted her shoulder. 'Don't worry, Anne, I wouldn't have done it if I hadn't thought it might work out for the best.'

She flinched away from his touch, too upset to care what he thought.

His voice drained of emotion, David said harshly, 'I'm not about to rape you. Not that I ever have—you've always been more than willing, haven't you?'

'And if not you just apply a little brute force, don't you?' she said nastily.

'There'll be no repetition of last night. I'm not so desperate for a woman that I'll go where I'm not wanted.'

'You always used to find plenty who wanted you. I hope you haven't lost your touch.'

'You little bitch! I'd like to throw you across my knee and spank you!'

'Brute force was the right phrase, wasn't it?' she said

steadily, even though she moved nearer to the door. He looked dangerous enough to try anything.

'Get out! And until Claire comes, just make sure you behave yourself while Jessica's around. The rest of the time, stay out of my sight!'

'It'll be a pleasure.'

She escaped to the kitchen and feverishly began to peel the vegetables, forcing her mind away from the angry man she had left in the study, and from his mother's impending visit. At least Deirdre and Terence were due back this evening, which should at least lessen the sense of enforced isolation with David. To think that only today she had told Jonathan that Stornaway was where she belonged—her rash statement must have tempted the gods to show just how fragile her security was.

The next morning Jessica decided to work on the snow fort, because she was hoping that the two younger Haley boys would be over for a visit later in the day. This fitted in well with Anne's plans since it would keep them both out of David's sight. They worked away industriously, moving what seemed to Anne like immense piles of snow. Then Jessica started to stockpile neat rows of snowballs, while Anne added chunks of frozen snow to the walls. About halfway through the morning she went into the house to get some dry mittens.

At the kitchen door she collided head-on with David. 'Sorry,' she gasped, raising a face pink-cheeked from the cold. Her eyes had taken on the brilliant green of her ski suit and tasselled cap, and her hair fell in lustrous waves over the collar. As though impelled by some force greater than his will, he pushed a shining strand back from her face; the hair was alive with electricity.

'We always did strike sparks off each other, didn't we?' he said ruefully.

Although despising herself for her weakness, she was painfully glad to have him talking to her again. 'We were young,' she said lightly.

'The implication being that we're older and wiser now?'

She was getting into deep waters. 'I—I don't know. Er—have you see Jessica's other mittens? The ones she has on are soaked.'

Dryly he said, 'They're right in front of you.'

Blushing, she picked them up. 'I'd better get back out and see what she's up to. This snow fort seems to be developing into a combination of the Eiffel Tower and Fort Knox!'

David's laugh was still ringing in her ears as she let herself out of the front door and started to walk across the driveway to the slope where the snow fort was located—strategically, she hoped. She heard the well-bred purr of the Mercedes and saw Terence coming down the hill. He must have been getting some groceries.

Then her heart stopped. Jessica had seen her coming and had left the snow fort; she was running towards the driveway, hidden from Terence's view by a snowbank that the plough had heaped up.

'Stop!' Anne yelled. 'Jessica, stop!' But the wind blew her words away. Frantically Anne waved a warning to Terence, then she dug her boots into the snow and began to run. From the corner of her eye she saw that Terence had put on the brakes. But the driveway was icy and the big car began skidding down the hill. Jessica was running right into its path. As though in slow motion Anne saw the child's terrified face.

In a burst of speed Anne would not have believed herself capable of, she too ran in front of the Mercedes and with all her strength flung Jessica into the snowbank. Something struck her shoulder, tumbling her to the ground and rolling her over and over. Smothered in snow and totally disorientated, she lay still.

Dimly she heard voices. Terence's brogue, thin and shaken. 'The wee girl—is she all right? God, I though I'd hit her!'

Then Jessica's screams, too piercing for hurt, more indicative of fear and outrage. And David's deep accents, calm and soothing. 'It's okay, Jess, you're not hurt. Hush now and just stay there with Terence a minute.'

Then she was being turned over with exquisite care, and David was exclaiming, 'Anne! My God, Anne, are you all right?' There was a note in his voice she had never heard before and hazily she opened her eyes, blinking up at him.

'Jess?' she said weakly. 'Did she get hurt?'

'No—there's not a mark on her, thanks to you. You saved her life.'

She tried to sit up and the world whirled around her, a kaleidoscope of white snow and blue sky. She clung to David, her forehead resting on his sleeve, her breath coming in short gasps.

'Where are you hurt?' he said matter-of-factly, although the hand he raised to her face was visibly shaking.

'I—don't think I am. Just dizzy.'

'I'm going to carry you to the house and call the doctor.'

She tried to protest, but her voice didn't seem to be working. She felt herself being picked up. They went into the house, David carrying Anne, and Terence following with a subdued Jessica crying quietly into his shoulder. Gently David deposited Anne on her bed and pulled a thick eiderdown over her. 'I'll let the doctor undress you, in case anything's broken. Just lie still, he'll be here in a few minutes.' She felt him sit on the edge of the bed and opened her eyes to see him taking the sobbing child from Terence. 'Okay, I've got her. Terence, this is an order—go down to the study and pour yourself a stiff brandy. You're as white as a ghost.'

'I—I'm sorry, sir. For what happened.'

'Nothing that happened was your fault,' David said with absolute conviction. 'You didn't even know Jessica was there. She's learned a lesson the hard way. Now do as I say, Terence, and then get Deirdre to make you a strong cup of tea with lots of sugar.'

Anne was touched by David's genuine concern for the older man and pleased that he had not blamed Terence for the near-tragedy. It had been nobody's fault. Just one of those accidents of timing that would have altered their lives irrevocably if she, Anne, hadn't got to Jessica in time.

Jessica's little voice said raggedly, 'Is Anne hurt?'

'I don't think so, pet. But the doctor's coming, just in case.'

There was a dull ache in Anne's shoulder and she felt desperately cold, unable to stop the shuddering of her limbs. As she closed her eyes to try and bolt out that nightmare image of Jessica in the path of the car, she drifted into a semiconscious daze. Then she heard Deirdre say, 'They're in here, Dr MacKinnon.'

'David, I gather there's been a bit of an accident. I had a chat with Terence downstairs—in fact, I gave him a tranquiliser to settle him down. Now, young miss Jessica, how are you?'

Anne opened her eyes. Dr MacKinnon was a heavy-set balding man in his fifties whose engaging grin and shrewd blue eyes inspired immediate confidence. She watched as he conducted a swift but thorough examination of Jessica; afterwards he pulled an orange lollipop out of his pocket and said, 'Go downstairs with Deirdre now, Jessica, and I expect to find the lollipop all gone by the time I come down.'

Jessica giggled, sounding more like herself, and something tight-held in Anne relaxed; she had been worried about the after-effects of the accident on Jessica. She saw that the doctor had turned his attention to her and managed to smile.

'You didn't tell me your wife had come back,' Dr MacKinnon said mildly to David.

For once Anne saw that David was completely nonplussed, so she said weakly, 'We've been keeping it quiet— even from Jessica for now.'

If the doctor thought this odd, he did not say so. Skilfully he eased her out of her ski suit and slacks, then cut away her sweater, leaving her only with a diminutive lace bra and panties. His hands were firm and gentle as he conducted his examination, and finally he pulled the eiderdown back over her. 'You're going to have a whopper of a bruise on your shoulder and it'll be sore for a few days, but there's nothing broken. You're a very fortunate, as well as a very brave, young woman. Now I'll leave David to get you into your nightclothes and then I want you to take this tablet with some hot milk. You'll sleep the night through and that's the best thing for you. I'll let myself out, David— I have to check on the state of your daughter's lollipop on the way.' He raised a hand in salute and they heard his footsteps diminishing down the stairs.

David got a clean nightdress from the drawer and helped Anne into a sitting position. As his fingers fumbled with the front closure of her bra, she glanced up. He was still white about the mouth, his face pale with strain. She must have made an involuntary movement, for his hands slid around to her back and wordlessly he held her close, his cheek resting against her hair; she could hear the laboured beating of his heart. Eventually he released her and looking deep into her eyes said, 'Thank you, Anne. That's all I can say. It doesn't bear thinking what might have happened if you hadn't been there. Dr MacKinnon was right—you were incredibly brave.'

Puzzled, she answered, 'No, I wasn't brave. I didn't even stop to think.' With an air of explaining the obvious she went on, 'Jessica's my child and she was in danger. I acted instinctively, I suppose. Any mother would have done the same. . . .'

She faltered to a stop because David was staring at her with a kind of desperate intensity, and again she sensed a question in his eyes. Frightened for no reason that she could think of, she shivered reminiscently. 'Sorry,' he muttered. 'You must be cold.' His hands brushed her flesh as impersonally as the doctor's as he undid her bra and helped her into her nightdress. There was a discreet tap on the door, and Deidre said, 'Here's the glass of hot milk that Dr MacKinnon said you'd be wanting, dearie. And Jessica would like to say goodnight before you settle down.'

Obediently Anne swallowed the pill that David held out to her and gulped the milk. She was already lying down when Jessica sidled in the door. The remnants of fear were still to be seen in Jessica's unusual pallor and wobbly bottom lip. Anne said soothingly, 'Why don't you come and lie down with me until I go to sleep? Then your daddy can take you down for supper.'

Like an arrow to the gold, Jessica huddled into Anne's arms. Anne's last memory before sleep overcame her was of David's face gazing down at two heads on the pillow, that same unanswered question imprinted on his face.

Claire arrived on the mid-afternoon flight two days later. David and Jessica went to meet her, Anne using her shoulder as an excuse to stay home. It was still sore, although it looked worse than it felt, for she had a huge discoloured bruise down her side.

She dressed with considerable care that afternoon, choosing a classically styled shirtwaister dress in a warm rust shade that brought out the auburn lights in her hair; it was a flattering dress and she knew it. She added a gold necklace and earrings that David had given her on their first anniversary, and allowed her hair to fall loosely over her shoulders. A pair of high-heeled shoes with thin open straps completed the outfit. As she observed herself in the mirror before going downstairs, she knew she looked as different from the Anne of four or five years ago as she possibly could, and this gave her added confidence. She was not the same girl whom Claire had manipulated and criticised, nor would she allow herself to be treated that way again ... fine resolutions, that quavered a bit as she heard the slam of the car doors outside and knew Claire had arrived. She waited in the living-room, her mouth suddenly dry.

'Ah, there you are, Anne,' said David, his eyes missing not one detail of her appearance. 'You look very lovely, my dear,' and he walked over and kissed her full on the mouth.

She glared at him indignantly, his tall body hiding her from anyone else's view. That kiss had been for Claire's benefit, she was sure. She'd show him! She wound her arms around his neck and pulled his head down, wickedly nibbling his lips with her teeth: 'You seemed to be gone a long time, darling,' she said huskily.

She saw the smothered laughter in his eyes as, too low for other ears, he murmured, 'You'll pay for that!' Then, more loudly, 'Come and say hello to Claire.'

Anne walked forward to meet her, hand held out, and as they uttered the conventional greetings, the two women surveyed each other in silence. Anne knew she herself had changed, but she was unprepared for the change in Claire. She was no longer the ramrod-straight, cold-eyed martinet whom Anne had feared so greatly. She had shrunk somehow. Her face had a network of new lines in it. There was almost a placatory look in her eye when she spoke, saying uncertainly, 'Hello, Anne, it's nice of you to have me here.'

Anne refrained from saying that she had had no choice in the matter. She remembered how earlier David had tried to warn her that Claire had changed—and she had disregarded him. She should have paid more attention, she thought grimly, wondering what on earth had caused such a transformation. Illness, perhaps? Surely not loneliness ... Claire had never had a lonely moment in her life.

Deirdre arrived with a tea tray, and the conversation limped along. Jessica was slowly becoming less shy of her grandmother; in spite of herself, Anne was touched to see the two of them talking together, Claire's face lit by pride ... could it even be love? Totally confused, Anne busied herself with pouring the tea.

Apparently Claire had not visited David at Stornaway before, so after tea he took her on a tour of the house, Jessica going with them. Anne wandered over to the window and looked out. It had started to snow, a myriad tiny flakes falling purposefully from the sky. In the dim grey light the outlines of the trees were softened and blurred. The same thing had happened to Claire, Anne thought whimsically. In a moment of insight she knew Claire no longer had the power to harm her. For four long years she had hated the other woman; now, miraculously, that hatred had evaporated, transformed to something akin to pity.

They ate formally in the dining room, Jessica wearing the new red dress that Claire had brought her from Montreal. Because David kept the conversation on matters of general interest, the dinner went well, although Anne was still glad to excuse herself to supervise Jessica's bath and bedtime ritual. When she went back downstairs she found David and Claire in the study, seated in the armchairs by the fire. She accepted a liqueur from David with a little smile of thanks and sat down on the couch. Her nerve ends were quivering, for there was an indefinable atmosphere of tension; the room seemed claustrophobic and she wished she could be anywhere else but where she was.

CHAPTER ELEVEN

I<small>T</small> was Claire who broke the silence. 'I have to talk to both of you,' she said. As Anne watched, she saw Claire's chin tilt with something of the old arrogance. 'It won't be pleasant.'

David shifted slightly in his chair, although he said nothing. He had expected something like this, Anne thought with sudden clarity. What was he hoping to hear? What he was likely to hear, she thought bitterly, was yet another cataloguing of all the reasons why he should not have married Anne. That had been a favourite ploy of Claire's. . . .

'I'll have to begin a number of years ago,' Claire said emotionlessly. 'I was always very ambitious for David. I wanted him to marry a girl of good family with money and social connections, but instead he met and fell in love with you, Anne. You were a penniless student nurse, an orphan who'd never had a proper home—you were the last person I wanted as a member of the family. But David was infatuated with you and he'd always been headstrong, and before I knew it, you were married.' She stared down at the diamonds that glittered coldly on her fingers.

'I always knew you resented me,' Anne interjected. 'But I was the one David wanted and I thought you would come to accept that in time.'

'You couldn't have been more wrong. I became obsessed with the idea of getting rid of you, because I was sure that sooner or later David would come to his senses and realise what a mess he'd made of his life by his impetuous marriage. So I encouraged you to go to parties without David, and I got invitations for him that didn't include you. I dropped hints to you, Anne, that David was seeing other women. And then you went on that skiing weekend. . . .'

174

As though he could no longer sit still, David thrust the poker into the fire, sending a shower of sparks up the chimney. He remained standing there, his eyes trained on his mother's face, his big body taut and still.

'I know you went with a group of young people, only one of whom was Ralph Stevenson. But I gave David the impression that you spent the weekend alone with Ralph at the chalet—I knew that would make him angry.' She paused, taking a sip of liqueur. 'And it did. But then something happened that I couldn't control. You became pregnant, Anne, and the two of you seemed as close as you'd ever been. I was furious, because I knew once you had a child David would never divorce you. I did all I could to cast doubts on the child's paternity, suggesting that Ralph could equally well have been the father——'

'You hated Anne that much?' David interrupted incredulously.

His mother looked at him steadily, although Anne noticed how tightly her hands were clenched in her lap. 'There's worse to come,' she said, and for the first time her voice faltered. 'You went away, David, just before the baby was due. Do you remember?'

'I'm not likely to forget it,' he said grimly.

'You left me with strict instructions to get in touch with you the minute Anne went into labour so that you could get home in time to be with her.'

'You did that, David?' Anne asked wonderingly.

'Yes—did you really think I'd leave you alone then?' He bit off the words.

Claire went on as if they had not spoken. 'I disregarded those instructions completely. Anne became ill and she had to go to hospital several days early. The baby—Jessica— was born five days before the date the doctor had given you, and afterwards Anne was more or less delirious for several days. Jessica was brought home and I hired a nurse to look after her. Once Anne was well enough to understand, I told her the baby had died——'

Anne had covered her face with her hands, remembering the agony of that day, so she did not see the anger blazing in David's eyes.

'I also told her you were finished with her, David, that you never wanted to see her again. And then I went home and waited to see what would happen. I was not at all surprised when they phoned me from the hospital and said Anne had left. I had the feeling that was what she would do.' Almost as though forcing herself to go on, she said wearily, 'So I telephoned you, David, and told you Anne had left you and would never come back. She wanted no part of the marriage—or of the child.'

Stunned, Anne stared at Claire, as everything fell into place. David had not lied to her about the child—Claire had. And it was Claire who had made sure David would not want his wife back. No wonder his love had turned to ashes!

'So I'd succeeded,' Claire said stonily. 'Anne was gone, and David had Jessica. And that's where all my plans went wrong. Because Jessica changed everything. From the start, I loved her so much. But she looked so like you, Anne —the likeness was a continual reproach to me. As the months passed and I saw how much David loved his daughter, and how bitterly he was hurt by your absence, I began to realise I'd done wrong. I'd treated you like puppets, not like people. And there was nothing I could do to put things right. You'd disappeared without a trace, Anne, and you never got in touch with us—why should you, after all? You didn't even know of Jessica's existence.'

'I'm finding this hard to believe,' David said evenly. 'You allowed Anne to think her child had died and her husband had rejected her. So for four years, Anne didn't even know she had a daughter. God, Claire, how could you?' He turned to Anne. 'You saw the advertisement— that's how you found out?'

Anne nodded. Her throat felt as though it was being squeezed in a giant vice and speech was beyond her.

'I know I did a dreadful thing,' Claire cried. 'But I've paid for it over and over again, knowing there was nothing I could do to make things right. Until you called last week,

David, and told me Anne had come back. I knew then I
had to come here and tell you both the truth.' Two tears
coursed silently down her wrinkled cheeks. 'How can I say
I'm sorry? What I did was unforgivable.'

So that accounted for the change in Claire, Anne
thought. Jessica had taught Claire what it was to love, and
time had done the rest. She found her voice and said
quietly, 'Don't cry, Claire. It's over and done with now.'

'No, it must not be over and done with—don't you see?
The only way I'll ever be able to live with myself is if you
and David can find happiness together. I know you've lost
four years, but you're both young. You could start again.'

This plea from Claire was the last thing Anne had expected. 'You've lost four years,' Claire had said, and how
bitterly true that was. Overwhelmed by a sense of the
futility and waste of it all, Anne knew she had had four long
years of emptiness and pain, of grief for her child and her
lost marriage. And all for nothing. It need never to have
happened. And now Claire's confession had come too late,
for David no longer loved her. All too clearly she could
remember him saying, 'I loved you then.' She could hardly
blamed him for having changed: he had been as much deceived by Claire as she had been. But whether or not she
blamed him was immaterial. The cold hard fact was that
their marriage was dead, for marriage requires two people
who love each other. That she loved David was not enough.

Suddenly she could not bear it. She had to get away and
be alone. She got to her feet in one lithe movement and
ran for the door, slamming it shut behind her. Dimly she
heard David's voice cry her name, but even that could not
stop her. She raced down the hall to the kitchen, kicked
off her shoes and thrust her feet into boots, only dimly
aware that Rover was at her side. Grabbing her jacket from
the hook in the porch, with belated cunning she slid the
bolt on the door to the kitchen. Then she was outside and
running away from the house as though pursued. Its lights
glowed more and more dimly until the whirling snow
crystals finally obliterated them.

Staggering through the knee-deep snow, breathing in

harsh gasps, she stumbled on. Tree branches grabbed at
her sleeve with sharp fingers. She tripped over a hidden
rock and almost fell. Then the hillside sloped so steeply
that her own momentum carried her forward at breakneck
speed. Scarcely able to see in front of her, she slammed
into a tree trunk and her hoarse cry of shock was tossed
away by the uncaring wind. She sank to the ground, nursing her sore shoulder, sobbing with the pain. A black shape
materialised through the snow, and she suppressed a
shriek of alarm before she realised what it was. 'Rover!'
she cried, throwing her arms around his neck.

For the first time since her headlong flight from the
house, she came to her senses. Huddled under the tree, she
stared out into a world of black and white. Darkness and
snow, there was nothing else. The raw sea wind tugged at
her hair: it seized the snow and flung it into ghostly shapes.
She became aware that she was cold and wet ... and lost.
She had no idea which way to go to get back to the house.

A sob of fear broke from her lips. She must have been
mad to have rushed out into a blizzard in the dead of
night! Her fingers tightened on the dog's collar, for he
represented her only security. She pushed herself upright,
trying to still the shivers that racked her body. 'Home,
Rover,' she quavered. 'Take me home.' But even as she
spoke the dog pricked his ears, straining to hear something
inaudible to her. Then he lunged forward. Anne's hand
was torn from the collar and to her horror she saw him
disappear into the darkness. She staggered after him, but
she was too late—the storm had swallowed him up.

She turned to go back and even the tree trunk had
vanished. She was alone in a world of blinding snow and
bitter cold. Fighting down hysteria, she tried desperately to
think. If she went up the hill, she should at least be going
in the right direction. Downward could lead only to the
river; the thought of its icy waters made her shudder. She
started up the slope, dragging her leaden limbs, knowing at
some deep, instinctive level that she must keep moving. It
would be all too easy to sink into the snow in an exhausted

stupor that could have only one ending. . . .

A spruce bough slapped her face. Blinded, she stopped for breath, leaning against the rough bark for support, her eyes closed.

Something leaped up at her. Her eyes flew open and she saw it was Rover, his tail wagging, his tongue lolling out of his mouth. Then the darkness was split by the yellow beam of a torch, and she was gathered into David's arms. 'Thank God I've found you,' he muttered roughly. 'You little idiot —running away like that!'

It was heaven to be safe in his arms. 'How did you find me?'

'Rover. I called him with the dog whistle, and then he led me back to you.'

He picked her up and she protested weakly, 'You'll never be able to carry me all the way to the house.'

'We're only about a hundred yards away from it. You've probably been going around in circles.'

She shivered, burying her face in his jacket. She had heard too many stories of people who had frozen to death only feet from safety. . . .

Within minutes they had reached the house. Anne blinked in the light, hearing Deirdre and Claire exclaim over her soaked state. Then David's voice overrode them both. 'She's come to no harm. I'll take her upstairs and look after her. Mother, you look worn out—I think you should go to bed.'

'You're sure she'll be all right?' Claire persisted, such unaccustomed anxiety in her voice that Anne had to suppress a smile.

'I'm fine,' she murmured weakly. It seemed important for her to add, 'Claire, you know what we were talking about earlier—I'm sorry it all happened, but there's no point in blaming yourself any more. I—I don't think you resent me now, do you?'

'No, Anne, I don't. I only want you and David to be happy.'

That was another question altogether, Anne thought,

but there wasn't much sense in telling Claire that. 'Good-night,' she said, knowing that never again would she have to fear Claire.

'Goodnight, Anne.'

David insisted on carrying Anne upstairs, nor did she argue much. She felt drained of energy, as though she was floating disembodied somewhere in space, watching a tall, broad-shouldered man carry his wife upstairs to bed. How deceptive appearances could be, she thought sadly.

It was not until David had put her down that she realised where she was: in his bedroom. She looked around at the dark blue hangings and the white carpet, and at the vast bed that seemed to dominate the room. 'This isn't my room,' she said stupidly, her teeth chattering.

'Yes, it is,' he said with utter conviction in his voice. 'It's where you belong.'

A spasm of shivering shook her, and he said prosaically, 'The bathroom is through there. Have a hot shower.' He pulled his blue robe out of the cupboard. 'You can put this on. I'll light the fire, and go down and get you something hot to drink.'

'You're being very dictatorial,' she complained, striving for dignity but only managing to sound peevish.

David smiled at her, a smile that did funny things to her heart. 'Yes, I am, aren't I? Do as you're told.'

She lacked both the energy and the will to argue. Taking the blue robe from him, she went into the bathroom and closed the door. In the mirror she saw a wet, be-draggled creature, strands of hair plastered to her forehead, mascara smeared on her cheek. It galvanised her into action. Slipping out of her clothes, she turned on the shower and stepped under the hot needles of spray, feeling her tired muscles relax as she was enveloped in the steamy heat. She towelled herself dry and rubbed the worst of the wetness from her hair.

There was nothing to stop her from going back into the bedroom now ... as she stood quietly, she could hear the faint sounds of David's footsteps and guessed that he must be lighting the fire. Her mind was buzzing with questions. Why had he brought her to his room and what did he mean when he said she belonged there? Was she openly to be known as his wife now? But if he didn't love her, what kind of a future would they have? Trying to be philosophical about it, she reasoned that at least now he knew she had not wilfully abandoned him and Jessica. Squaring her shoulders, she took a deep breath and went into the bedroom.

'There you are,' he said casually, poking at the fire. 'Feel better?'

'Mmm—much.' She knelt down on the rug by the fireplace, holding out her hands to the blaze.

He put a glass of hot spiced wine on the hearth and went into the bathroom, coming back with a dry towel. 'Bend over, and I'll dry your hair.'

She leaned forward obediently and the wet strands of hair separated, baring the delicate nape of her neck. David began to rub her hair, his hands gentle, until it hung forward in burnished waves. 'It's dry now,' he said, and there was something in his voice that made her heart flutter in her breast.

She shook her hair back and said softly, 'Thank you.' She had no idea how beautiful she looked kneeling there, her skin white against his dark robe; it was far too big for her, drooping from the shoulders and emphasising the fragility of her wrists and hands.

'Are you warm enough?' asked David.

'Yes,' she answered truthfully, sensitive enough to his moods to know this wasn't what he had intended to say.

'You were very generous when you spoke to Claire in the kitchen.'

'Well, it's pretty obvious that she's sorry for what she did. When I first saw her I couldn't get over the change in her, but now I can understand it. I think she's paid for her meddling.'

'Meddling!' He laughed shortly. 'That's putting it mildly! I'll never forget that telephone call I had from her after Jessica was born—when she passed along the message that you were finished with our marriage, and that you'd disappeared from the hospital without a trace. I flew home on the first flight I could get. I saw Jessica—and even then she looked like you. And then I went to the hospital, and found out you'd been ill and could hardly have recovered before you left.'

He raked his fingers through his hair and then laid his hand on her knee, as though to reassure himself that she really was there. 'I nearly went mad in the next few days, picturing you ill and alone and unhappy. I called hotels and hospitals, I went to all the stations and the airports. I discovered that you'd been at Dorval from your credit card slip, but I couldn't find your name on any of the flight lists. You'd just dropped out of sight.'

His hand was still resting on her leg, and she placed her own on top of it in an unspoken gesture of comfort. 'And all the time I was in Halifax, not knowing a soul, and feeling utterly miserable.'

'I was sure you'd get in touch with me sooner or later. I thought you might have been depressed after the baby was born and needing to get away for a while, but that you'd be back. Every time the phone rang I thought it would be you. I haunted the post office. But nothing ever came. And the days became weeks and the weeks months, and I gradually came to realise that you really were finished with me. You'd meant what you said. I suppose that was when I started to hate you—it was the only way I could cope with it.'

'I felt much the same way,' Anne said sadly. 'But at least you had Jessica.'

'Yes, I had Jessica. But she was a constant reminder of you, because the older she got, the more she looked like you.'

'Her hair is just like yours, though,' Anne said softly, wishing she could reach up and stroke it.

'It is, isn't it? And that reminds me of how I'd accused you of making love with Ralph—I'd have given anything to have been able to take those words back.'

There was a silence. 'Why did you move here?' she asked curiously; she had often wondered about his reasons.

'I couldn't bear to stay in Montreal. Everywhere I went, every restaurant and theatre, we'd been together ... the house was full of memories—the dining-room where we'd eaten together, the living-room where we'd entertained friends, the bedroom where we'd slept together....'

He looked up and Anne blushed fierily. A spark leaped between them and he raised her hand to his lips, kissing her palm. With lazy grace he got to his feet and of necessity she stood up too. He drew her over to the bed and sat on the end of it, pulling her down in his lap. She could feel the warmth of his body through his thin shirt, and the hardness of his thighs against her legs. Her heart began to knock against her rib cage.

David nuzzled her neck with his mouth. 'You smell nice,' he murmured. 'Do you have any idea how distracting you are? What were we talking about?'

'Why you moved to the Island,' she said meekly, although her dancing eyes belied her voice.

'Yeah ... well, a friend of mine from Toronto owned Stornaway, and he'd heard I was thinking of leaving Montreal. So he got in touch with me and we came and looked at it. I liked it right away. I thought it would be a great place for Jessica to grow up—fresh air, space, beaches and horses in the summer, skiing in the winter. So I bought it. But once I moved here, I found I was away a lot, and it wasn't fair to expect Deirdre to look after Jessica. So I advertised—and you got the job.' He held her close, his arms like steel bands. 'Thank God you did!'

She said carefully, 'You must be glad to have me back for Jessica's sake.'

He raised his head, his eyes puzzled. 'Well, of course I am. But——'

'David, don't feel you have to pretend,' she said. Now that all the lies and deceptions from the past were in the open, she wanted only the truth between them—no matter if it wasn't what she wanted to hear. 'I know you don't love me now——'

'How do you know that?'

'You told me so yourself.'

'When?' he said blankly.

'One day when we were talking. You said, 'I loved you then,' so I know you don't love me any more. But that's all right. For Jessica's sake we can manage at least to be friends, can't we?' An appalling abyss suddenly opened in front of her. 'Unless you don't want to?' she faltered, wondering how she would bear it if he didn't.

He pulled her round so that she was facing him. 'Anne, we'd better get something straight——'

She flinched from the roughness of his voice. 'It's all right, I understand,' she whispered. 'People change, feelings change. After all that's happened, I could hardly expect you still to care for me——'

'Will you please be quiet for a minute!'

Wide-eyed, she gazed up at him. 'I . . . I'm sorry.'

'So you should be. Here I am trying to tell you that I love you and you keep on interrupting me.'

'You—love me?'

'Of course! I've never stopped loving you. Oh, I told myself I hated you. But the very intensity of my hatred sprang from loving you so much. You're in my bones and my blood, Anne. You're part of me and always will be.'

Almost frightened to believe him, she said, 'You didn't act like you loved me when I came back.'

'How could I? I didn't know why you'd come. I didn't understand this whole Miss Winters game. And on the whole you weren't exactly encouraging—apart from one night when you'd had too much to drink. Which wasn't exactly flattering to my ego!'

Incredibly she began to believe him. With mock crossness she said, 'I expect I'll be hearing about that night for the rest of my days!'

'I expect you will,' he rejoined cheerfully. Then his smile

faded and his eyes fastened intently on hers. 'Did you say for the rest of your days? Does that mean you'll stay, Anne?'

'I've been waiting for you to ask me,' she said demurely.

He looked down, a memory of pain flickering across his face, 'I was scared to ask you,' he said slowly. 'Scared that you'd say no.'

That her self-confident, arrogant David could so humble himself cut her to the quick. 'I want to live with you very much,' she said steadily.

'Can I hope that in time you'll learn to love me again?'

She cupped his face in her hands, her eyes overflowing with joy. 'Like you, I never stopped. Oh, David, David— I love you so much!'

Somehow she found herself flat on her back on the bed, with David's body lying over her as he rained kisses on her face and neck and shoulders. He pushed the robe open and with a deliberate sensuality that made her quiver, ran his mouth over the pink-tipped fullness of her breast. Wanting to feel his flesh against hers, she unbuttoned his shirt, moving her hands over the taut muscles of his chest and shoulders. She felt him fumbling with the waistband of his trousers and the sweet ache of desire flooded her limbs. . . .

Afterwards they lay back on the pillows, Anne cuddled into David's body, his arm around her shoulders. She marvelled at the difference those three little words—I love you—had made: she felt cherished and safe, as close to him as it was possible to feel with another human being. 'Do you remember when we made love before Claire came?' she murmured. 'I felt so lonely when I woke and found you'd gone.'

'You'll never have to feel that way again, I promise you. I'll always be with you when you need me.'

She ran her fingers along his rib cage, delighting in the smoothness of his skin. 'You know,' she said slowly, 'although it was dreadful while it was happening, maybe in the long run we'll have a better marriage because we've been apart. I learned a lot in those four years——'

'You changed from a young girl into a wise and beautiful woman.'

'Thank you,' she murmured, tears of sheer happiness in her eyes. She sought for the right words. 'I trust in your strength now. I know I can depend on you—you'll never let me down.'

'I feel the same way about you,' David said gently. 'In a very practical way that's what love's all about.' He leaned on one elbow, watching the firelight fllicker over her skin, and began to stroke the length of her body, as though memorising all its tantalising curves. 'Of course,' he added conversationally, 'love can be about this, too,' and he leaned forward to kiss her.

Before she surrendered to the surging pleasure of his lovemaking, she said, 'David, what'll we say to Jessica when she finds us in bed together tomorrow morning?'

She felt his frame shake with laughter. 'Let's just tell her you're her mother and you've come home to stay.'

'I wonder what she'll think of that.'

'Knowing Jessica, she'll probably say something like "That's good. I wanted Anne to stay for ever and ever." And that's what you're going to do.'

'Yes, David,' she murmured, 'for ever and ever.'

Give yourself and your friends a romantic Christmas.

First time in paperback, four superb romances
by favourite authors, in an attractive maroon and
gold gift pack. A superb present to give. And to receive.

Sandstorm	**Lord of the High Valley**
Anne Mather	Margaret Way
Man's World	**Enemy In Camp**
Charlotte Lamb	Janet Dailey

United Kingdom	£2.60
Rep. of Ireland	£2.86
Publication	10th October 1980

Look for this gift pack at your local Mills & Boon stockist.

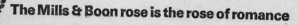

The Mills & Boon rose is the rose of romance

The Mills & Boon Rose is the Rose of Romance

Look for the Mills & Boon Rose next month

IMAGES OF LOVE *by Anne Mather*
Tobie couldn't resist seeing Robert Lang again, to exact her revenge — but she didn't know what had happened to Robert since they had last met ...

BRAND OF POSSESSION *by Carole Mortimer*
Jake Weston's lack of trust in her ought to have killed all the love Stacy felt for him — but it didn't.

DIFFICULT DECISION *by Janet Dailey*
Deborah knew that her job as secretary to the forceful Zane Wilding would be difficult — but the real challenge was to her emotions ...

HANNAH *by Betty Neels*
Nurse Hannah Lang was happy to accompany the van Eysink's back to Holland, but the unbending Doctor Valentijn van Bertes was not quite so enthusiastic about it.

A SECRET AFFAIR *by Lilian Peake*
As a confidential secretary, Alicia was well aware how essential it was to keep secret about her boss's new project. So why didn't he trust her?

THE WILD MAN *by Margaret Rome*
Rebel soon realised how Luiz Manchete had earned his name — the wild man — when she found herself alone with him in the heart of his jungle kingdom ...

STRANGER IN THE NIGHT *by Charlotte Lamb*
When Clare met Macey Janson, she began to lose some of her fear of men. So why did Luke Murry have to turn up again, making Macey suspect the worst of her?

RACE AGAINST LOVE *by Sally Wentworth*
Toni disliked Adam Yorke intensely, and her friend Carinna was more than welcome to him! But did Toni *really* mean that?

DECEPTION *by Margaret Pargeter*
Sick to death of being run after for her money, Thea ran away herself — but she only found a new set of problems ...

FROZEN HEART *by Daphne Clair*
Joining an expedition to the Antarctic, Kerin was taken aback to discover that the arrogant Dain Ransome was to be its leader ...

If you have difficulty in obtaining any of these books from your local paperback retailer, write to:

Mills & Boon Reader Service
P.O. Box 236, Thornton Road, Croydon, Surrey, CR9 3RU.

Available November 1980

Doctor Nurse Romances

and October's
stories of romantic relationships behind the scenes
of modern medical life are:

SURGEON'S CHALLENGE
by Helen Upshall

Sister Claire Tyndall's success as a nurse was undoubted
— but as a woman? Richard Lynch and Dr Alan Jarvis
both made it clear that they were interested in her. Both
were handsome and determined, but both — unfortunately
for Claire — seemed to be married already!

ATTACHED TO DOCTOR MARCHMONT
by Juliet Shore

Doctor Sally Preston's relationship with her new chief,
Darien Marchmont, got off to a sticky start. So she was
less than pleased to discover that their first joint
assignment was a two-man medical survey in the heart
of the North African desert!

Mills & Boon Classics

The very best of Mills & Boon
romances, brought back for those of you
who missed reading them when they
were first published.

In
October
we bring back the following four
great romantic titles.

NO QUARTER ASKED
by Janet Dailey
Stacy Adams was a rich girl who wanted to sample real life for
a change, so she courageously took herself off alone to Texas
for a while. It was obvious from the first that the arrogant
rancher Cord Harris, for some reason, disapproved of her — but
why should she care what he thought?

MIRANDA'S MARRIAGE
by Margery Hilton
Desperation forced Miranda to encamp for the night in Jason
Steele's office suite, but unfortunately he found her there, and
after the unholy wrath that resulted she never dreamed that a
few months later she would become his wife. For Jason was
reputed to be a rake where women were concerned. So what
chance of happiness had Miranda?

THE LIBRARY TREE
by Lilian Peake
Carolyn Lyle was the niece of a very influential man, and
nothing would convince her new boss, that iceberg Richard
Hindon, that she was nothing but a spoiled, pampered darling
who couldn't be got rid of fast enough! Had she even got time
to make him change his mind about her?

PALACE OF THE POMEGRANATE
by Violet Winspear
Life had not been an easy ride for Grace Wilde and she had
every reason to be distrustful of men. Then, in the Persian
desert, she fell into the hands of another man, Kharim Khan,
who was different from any other man she had met . . .